Now Scott was chasing after Kevin, who had just taken possession of the ball. Flinging himself forward, he managed to grab him around the waist. Kevin's bare feet slipped on the wet grass and he came tumbling down with Scott on top of him.

What Mike saw next shot through him like lightning.

Scott and Kevin started to kiss. Wrapping their muscular arms around each other, the two of them squirmed in the damp grass and began to grind their hips together.

MIKE AND ME

ANONYMOUS

A BADBOY BOOK

First BADBOY Edition 1992

Second Printing January 1996

ISBN 1-56333-419-4

Cover Photograph © 1996 Sean Kahlil

Cover Design by Dayna Navaro

Manufactured in the United States of America
Published by Masquerade Books, Inc.
801 Second Avenue
New York, N.Y. 10017

CHAPTER ONE

I

It wasn't his original reason for joining the Edison Community College gymnastics squad, but Mike Belson was finding that just being within towel-snapping distance of the dozen or so truly hot-looking guys he'd met on the team made it all worth while; not to mention the effect that the constant grueling workouts were having on his body. At eighteen, when he had joined the team, he had been just five-foot-five and weighed in at a skinny one hundred twenty pounds. After three years of continuous training, though, Mike had shot up to a Johnny-come-lately five-eleven and built his frame into one hundred seventy-five pounds of solid, sculpted muscle.

With that fantastic body, and his soft, brown, puppy-dog eyes, the short crop of bleached-blond hair that topped the chiseled features of his face, he was easily one of the best-looking guys in his school.

He loved being the center of attention, catching raps with girls in front of the other guys, standing as the workout mate of choice for most of the gymnasts after class. In fact, with schoolwork coming easy to him, personal problems few and far between, and a team closing in on the regional championships, Mike's absolute favorite pastime these days was checking out the other studs on the squad.

The first one to catch his eye as the team made its way to the locker room after one particular day's practice was Dave Sommers. Dave, like Mike, was also a junior on the team. They had signed up with the squad at around the same time. Mike had stolen many long moments of sheer pleasure ever since watching him grow into his currently very hot body. The light blond hair of Dave's younger days had darkened considerably, and his hazel eyes looked out from perpetually sleepy lids capped with dark, heavy eyebrows.

His body wasn't bad either, Mike decided as he covertly watched Dave peel out of his soaking gymnast's tank that day. His firm, hairless chest sparkled with perspiration brought on by an unusually excruciating workout. It rose and fell with each steady breath he took, and the muscles in his arms worked smoothly as he slowly pulled the tank over his head. The thick tufts of hair beneath his muscular arms were matted to his skin, and he turned his gaze up as he sniffed and wiped the sweat from his nose with the back of his hand.

Mike had to turn his head back to his own locker to prevent eye contact, and an imminent hard-on from developing in his shorts. He would miss the one quick movement Dave made as he pulled both his shorts and jock-strap down from his hard, round ass, but he swore he could hear the sound Dave's heavy cock made as it pulled free to slap against his muscular thigh.

"Hey, Mike, you gonna shower?" Dave asked.

"Uh, yeah, just a second."

"Well, get your head out of your locker and come on."

Dave threw his towel over his shoulder and strolled nonchalantly toward the shower with his big dick flopping back and forth between his beautifully developed legs.

Mike got control of himself, stripped off his gym suit, and followed after Dave.

When he reached the showers, he immediately turned his face into the cool spray of the water, letting his aching body soak in sheens of wet relief before slipping a bar of soap over his hard chest and stomach.

As the lather began to develop, Mike chanced a glance over to his left to see who was next to him. It turned out to be one of the seniors on the team, Jason Carmichael. Jason was the squad's resident golden boy. Not only was he the best gymnast on the team, but he also came from a rich family and was graced with a beautiful face that somehow held captive the angelic innocence of his days as an altar boy at St. Luke's.

Jason Carmichael, however, was anything but innocent. He was sought after by practically every girl at Edison, and there were more than a few from the neighboring university whom he was rumored to have blessed with his holy screwdriver. Running his eyes down to the huge piece of meat hanging between Jason's legs, Mike couldn't help feeling envious of those girls.

Just as he was turning back to lean into the cool, soothing streams of water, Mike was suddenly grabbed by his naked ass, and it startled the hell out of him.

"Jesus Christ!" The bar of soap shot out of Mike's hand.

"Better watch those roving peepers, dude."

Mike turned around to see the grinning face of his best friend and fellow gymnast, John Wallach, whose eyes sparkled with mischief as he laughed at his buddy's reaction.

"God, you scared the shit out of me!" Mike said as he playfully shoved John away.

"Well, next time don't let yourself get so distracted. People will talk, you know."

"Yeah, when monkeys fly out of my butt, bud." Mike kept a poker grin, only to find himself getting distracted again, but then he always did when he was around John.

Mike loved guys. For as long as he could remember, he had been turned on by hot-looking men. He had never really stopped to analyze his feelings, except that he knew in no uncertain terms that he had to keep his desires to himself. Everyone seemed to think he was super-swift with women, and that he just didn't brag about it. That suited him fine. It was why he wasn't at all spooked by John's "people will talk" comment. It was just one of your basic little secret facts: dudes turned him on. Young, athletic, muscular guys like himself, and the hottest guy of all—his number-one turn-on—happened to be none other than his best friend, John Wallach.

John's hot body made Mike almost instinctively begin to salivate. The dark-haired stud had moved back into his own shower, and his eyes closed as he let the spray of water rinse the soap bubbles down the smooth slopes of his body. The water sluiced over the steep curve that flowed from his taut, bulging chest to his trim, well-muscled stomach, and washed down over his his tight, dimpled ass, his sinewy thighs and rock-hard calves. His perpetually semi-erect eight-inch-long cock cut through the flow, with its always intriguing upward curl and the small patch of dark pubic hair that surrounded it.

Mike just barely got control of himself and slipped out of the shower, wrapping a towel tightly around his waist, securing his springy cock while John finished rinsing.

"Hey, Mike, I think the set of weights and the rest of that workout equipment my dad bought me is gonna be delivered tonight." John stepped out of the shower and began to dry himself off. "If I get it all set up, what would you think of coming over tomorrow night and going through a little workout with me?"

"That'd be great!" Mike lit up. Any occasion for the two of them to get together was good enough for him, especially if it involved bare skin and sweat. "Where are you planning on setting it up?"

"I was thinking of keeping it in the garage. At least until winter. I hate it when people come stomping through my sessions. I like to concentrate. I need privacy."

Mike nodded his head. Privacy had become the year's biggest issue at his house, and as he dressed he decided it was going to be real important that he have some as soon as he got back home and into his bedroom.

He told John that if the equipment came he would be over tomorrow night. Then, after a chummy slap on the shoulder, he turned and headed out of the locker room.

When he got home, he wasted no time. He made a thorough check of the house to make sure he was alone. His mother and father were, as usual, still at work, and his live-in second cousin, Kevin, must be at wrestling practice back at Edison.

Satisfied that he had the house to himself, Mike ran up the steps four at a time to his room. Slipping inside, he shut and locked the door behind him.

Blue jeans, pullover sweaters, and sports gear were strewn about in random piles across the plushly carpeted floor of the room. Pennants and posters of his favorite teams and athletes, some up there since he was a kid, were taped to the walls. Last year's *Sports Illustrated* swimsuit issue cover model was strategically positioned across from the door, a curvaceous token of sound mind and healthy body to family and friends. Mike surveyed it all, searching for where he'd casually hidden a small plastic bottle of baby oil, before starting to run his fingers slowly up and down over his chest and stomach.

"God, I love this," he murmured, half-grinning into the silver-backed mirror above his oaken chest of drawers. Languidly, he began to unbutton the untucked, oversized flannel shirt he'd worn to class that morning; the one that, despite the way it stiffly draped around him, could never completely disguise the beautiful body it covered.

As the last button came free, he slowly drew the fingertips of both hands back up over the exposed flesh of his stomach and chest, causing goosebumps to appear on his otherwise flawless skin. A trembling sigh escaped from his lips, and he finished off the caress with a simultaneous tweak of both his nipples, which had become hard in just the past few seconds. Only then, with a shrug, did he slip the shirt from his powerful shoulders, letting it fall to the ground in a rumpled heap.

The cool air of his bedroom came as a tingling shock to his skin, a wintry contrast to the warm sweaty atmosphere of the locker room. The shock of it only hastened his mind back to the gym at Edison and the gorgeous-looking guys he had just been with at practice. His right hand inched down until it caressed the head of the already-rigid erection in his jeans, while his left hand continued to run over his marvelous torso. Through it all, his mind raced with visions of his rock-hard teammates.

He began to rub his thickening cock through the heavy denim material of his jeans as he tried to imagine Dave Sommers at home doing the same thing to himself. He allowed a soft moan to escape his lips as he pictured Dave rubbing the bulging jock-strap which only barely contained his throbbing dick. By Mike's calculation it had to be at least nine inches long.

His mind quickly did a flip, as his rubbing became more forceful and urgent, and he was now watching the beautiful and big-dicked Jason Carmichael being sucked off by some faceless girl. Her mouth went up and down on the ten-inch shaft, causing it to become slicker and stiffer with every stroke. God, she'd barely be able to get him down her throat in a minute! Now a layer of sweat was forming on Jason's body, causing his skin to take on the same shiny gloss as his spit-soaked cock. Then the girl was gone and her face was replaced by Mike's own, and it was his mouth, clearly this time, sliding up and down on Jason Carmichael's incredible shaft.

The image started to fade, a bit too quickly for Mike's taste. As he got older, he'd found it harder to maintain vivid fantasies, and he figured that the reason for this was either because TV was giving him a shorter attention span; or, much more likely, because he was getting tired of daydreaming and a bit too eager to make all these crazy thoughts a reality.

He unbuttoned the top of his Levi's, delicately pulled the zipper down, and held his breath as he scooted the tight jeans past his thighs. All the while, he refrained from touching the turgid flesh that was the most sensitive area of his body. He stepped out of the denim at his ankles and mused at his wildly distended underwear. Out of the corner of his eye, he saw himself in the mirror and almost giggled. It looked like G.I. Joe dolls had pitched a big Fruit of the Loom tent between his hips. He shivered as his hand slowly reached down to touch it. His fingers ran lightly over the cotton, from the bottom of his balls all the way up the stalk to the place on his underwear where a wet spot was already starting to form. The exquisite feeling was a pleasant contrast to the rough treatment his cock had been receiving while still in his jeans, and his skin tingled with the sensation.

Now his mind was drifting again as his fingers caressed the stiff joint beneath the stretchy fabric. He was envisioning John Wallach standing in that shower, running the soap over himself, drawing it into his armpits, and up the crack of his ass. This time, however, Johnny-boy had begun to play with that semierect dick of his, slicking it up with suds and coaxing it to full hardness. As the head continued to expand, the ever-present curve of his shaft became more pronounced, as if it were trying to reach up and touch his bellybutton. At its throbbing fullest, it wouldn't be far from succeeding, either. The thick, curving stalk was capped with a fat, plum-shaped head. His balls dangled low from the heat of the shower, and they brushed against his sparsely haired, thickly muscled thighs.

Mike began to rub his rock-hard cock more vigorously, his right shoulder and biceps pumping and flexing smoothly. He pulled up and down while imagining John doing the same. He imagined him closing his eyes with pleasure as he experienced the double sensations of the water spraying down on his back and his hand pistoning up and down on his cock. Abandoning himself to the fantasy, starting to lose control, Mike finally pulled his underwear down his legs. His magnificent erection briefly got caught in the elastic waistband, then snapped up and slapped against the flesh of his belly, eager to be stroked into a furious explosion.

Jumping onto his bed, Mike pulled himself up against the headboard and paused to survey the prominent display before him. He spread his legs wide to admire the thick and heavy eight inches of prime beef as it jutted toward his pecs, like an arrow, perfectly straight from the thick bush of dark blond pubic hair that surrounded it.

He traced his finger up the thin line of hair that inched its way up to his navel. The piss slit at the head of his cock flared violently as it became soaked with his pre-cum. Reaching a finger down to it, he gathered up what he could of the fluid and then brought it up to his face. He passed the heady liquid beneath his nose and then, taking another one of his patented self-dares, proceeded to lick the pre-cum from his finger. The taste made him shiver, and his cock became stiffer than he could ever remember.

He spit into his palm and used it to slick up his erection before he began stroking it more rapidly, his hand now flashing back and forth as his mind returned to John in the shower. John was leaning backward now, and his knees were slightly bent as the water continued to spray him down. The position was causing the corded muscles of his legs to stand out prominently as his hand flew up and down on his cock.

Mike matched those movements on his own cock while his free hand reached down to the lightly

15

furred track that ran from beneath his balls to the crack of his ass. His finger found its way to the tight sphincter muscle of his virgin asshole and began to work its way inside. His hips began to rise off the bed as his finger worked its way in deeper, and his head starting rolling back and forth on his powerful neck as the pleasure continued to heighten and become unbearable.

In his fantasy, John was also almost at the point of losing it. Every muscle of his body was standing at attention as Mike's gym buddy neared his orgasm. John's teeth clenched and his lips parted to reveal them, and his free hand reached up to grasp the head of the shower for support. Then his mouth opened suddenly and let out a long gasping moan—he was coming! First, one long, stringy jet of thick cum shot up and out of his incredibly stiff, upturned cock. The next spasm shot out even farther, followed in quick succession by two smaller, weaker bursts. Mike envisioned his best friend's salty, white cum swirling around on the floor of the shower stall, then running down the big drain in the center of the room.

That was all it took for Mike. He grabbed firmly onto his cock, shoved his finger all the way up his ass, lifted his body almost completely off the bed, and let out a shuddering moan as he began to erupt. Stream after white-hot stream burst from his massive cock-head, to shoot up over his chest and into the crook of his neck. The third burst missed his body altogether and landed against the headboard behind him. Two more smaller shots landed on his chest and stomach before he finished firing his load.

After taking a minute to catch his breath, Mike looked down at his cum-splattered torso. He took his fingers, wiped some of the warm, sticky fluid off his firm torso, and greedily stuck them into his mouth—yet another dare accomplished. He meticulously continued to perform this operation until he had swallowed all the cum he had so recently ejaculated.

He lay there a while, catching his breath, waiting for his heartbeat to return to normal before pulling his underwear on over his still-enlarged cock. Contented, he then turned over on his side and fell fast asleep.

About an hour later, the sound of his mother calling him and his second cousin to dinner caused him to jerk awake. The first thing he saw when he awoke was the shot of his cum that had dried on the headboard behind him. He laughed as he pulled on his clothes and then headed down to dinner.

CHAPTER TWO

CHAPTER TWO

II

The next evening was a Friday and everyone in the Belson family was in a hurry to finish dinner. Friday night was, traditionally, Marge Belson's night to play bridge and Richard Belson's night to play poker with the boys from the office. Mike and Kevin were obviously pleased with this situation, as it gave them free rein to do as they pleased with the start of their weekend.

"So what are you boys planning to do with yourselves tonight?" Marge Belson asked in her best concerned-mother voice.

Kevin responded first. "I'm going over to Scott's to watch TV and spend the night."

Mike gave his cousin a knowing smile. He was able to translate that answer to mean that Kevin and his best friend, Scott Gorseth, would be out having a wild time on the town with no curfew to worry about.

Kevin was Richard Belson's first cousin's son.

He'd moved into the house last year after some trouble down south that no one liked to talk about. Everything had been just fine here ever since, and though Mike had his suspicions about what had happened, he guessed it didn't really matter. Kevin was a great guy, always so laid back and happy-go-lucky. Although the blood relation was rather thin, and there was a two-year age difference, they'd been like brothers since the day Kevin had moved in.

One thing was for certain: thanks to Mike's parents' Friday-night rituals, Kevin had been able to develop a reputation as one of the wildest partiers at Edison Community College, despite the fact that he was only a sophomore. Scott, best friend on the wrestling squad, had a pretty cool father who was hardly ever home, and together they made a good match.

"Well, that sounds nice!" Marge continued. "And what are you planning for tonight, dear?" she asked, turning to Mike.

"Oh, I'm just going over to John's. He just got a brand new set of workout equipment and I told him I'd help him set it up."

"Well, be sure you're home by one, Mike. I don't want a lot of noise when you get in, either," his father said.

"Okay, Dad." Not that Pop would know if he didn't. Richard Belson seldom got home from his poker games before two in the morning, and usually in no condition to be aware of what his grown son was up to.

After they finished the meal, Kevin helped Mrs. Belson clear the table and load the dishwasher. As soon as it was running, Marge took off, and Richard was not long in following.

"So what have you really got planned for

tonight?" Mike asked his cousin as soon as they were safely gone.

"Actually, I was telling the truth for a change," Kevin confessed with a shrug. "Scott's dad is out of town on business, so we're going to hang around his place tonight. Of course, we also have a bag of great pot and intend on getting massively stoned," he added with a smile.

"Ah, yes! Vitamin M!" Mike said with a laugh.

"How 'bout you? Any truth to the weights bit?"

"Yeah, I'm afraid so. I guess I'm just getting boring in my old age."

"Well, shit, man! If you feel like it, when you're done at John's, come on over to Scott's. There's more than enough pot to go around, and you know Scott would be happy to see you. Shit, he's always asking about you."

"Sounds great! Maybe I will. It depends on how long it takes to unpack the stuff." Something long and firm in Mike was hoping for other developments with his best friend, and some sly overture was coming to a slow simmer in his horny mind, but shit, that was just wishful thinking—and Scott sure was easy to look at.

"What's John need with workout gear, anyway?" Kevin asked. "I've never seen a dude with so many fucking muscles. If I had a build like that there'd be no stopping me on the wrestling mat!"

"Hell, you don't exactly have a feeble-looking body yourself." Mike laughed as he stood up and slapped his cousin on the back. "Listen, I might just take you up on your offer later on. Save me a jay."

The early October night had turned unseasonably warm at around sixty degrees. As he walked, Mike couldn't help thinking about what a sexy-looking dude Kevin was becoming. He thought back to just about a week ago when he had attended one of his cousin's wrestling meets. His mouth had literally hung open when he first saw Kevin stroll out onto the mat wearing his skintight wrestler's uniform. Mike had stared in disbelief as he surveyed the awesome body this mischievous little relative of his had developed. Kevin's torso didn't have the same kind of mass that was common to gymnasts like Mike, but he more than made up for it in the muscle-definition department. Mike's attention had been riveted as he watched Kevin flex his thickly muscled forearms, biceps, and triceps, stretching them behind his back, just barely exposing the dark blond tufts of hair beneath his arms.

Mike was even more impressed when Kevin began to do some deep knee bends. What always impressed Mike most about wrestlers was the massive legs they were able to develop, even more so than gymnasts—and his cousin was definitely no exception. The powerful, thick muscles bulged visibly, stretching out the leg openings of his Spandex uniform as he performed his warm-ups. Looking up, Mike noted with interest the contrast between Kevin's furry legs and the bare, flat pectorals of his chest—or at least what he could see of his cousin's chest before it sloped down under his uniform. Though they really were barely related, their bodies were similar—hairy legs and a practically bare torso except for some light fuzz—and that little fact had really begun to turn Mike on.

The most impressive thing about Kevin that night was what Mike saw so poorly disguised in the crotch of his skintight uniform. By all appearances, his cousin's dick was huge! It looked like it was at least six inches long when soft. It put Mike in a trance as Kevin wrestled, and he had only snapped out of it when the match was over. To his amazement, Kevin's dick looked even larger afterward. Mike only had a brief look, though, because his cousin quickly picked up a towel and held it in front of him as he walked back to his team's bench.

Mike was so turned on by the memory that he started to get a hard-on as he walked up the sidewalk to John's house.

He only had to wait a couple of seconds after ringing the doorbell for John to answer. All he was wearing was a tank top and a skimpy pair of running shorts that looked like they'd been outgrown about five years ago.

"Hey dude, glad you could make it!" He beamed as he ushered Mike into the house. "I've already gotten started putting this thing together in the garage. My parents are downstairs watching TV, so we shouldn't be bothered."

As they stepped into the garage, Mike couldn't help shaking his head, because the Wallachs' garage was anything but a chilly house for two-point-five cars. There were no vehicles stored in it, or lawn equipment, or recreational gear. It was more like just another room in the house. The main doors were all sealed shut, the floor was carpeted, and the place was well lighted. It came complete with a couch, tables, and a TV set. John had designed it as a personal rec room when his plans for a part-time job and a roommate off-campus had fallen through before the beginning of the term. Now he used the place almost constantly. His father'd told him that if he still couldn't afford to move out by Thanksgiving, the family would chip and and have the place insulated for the winter.

"This is what I've unpacked so far," John said as he waved his hand over a recently assembled bench press. "I thought this whole thing was going to be a snap but it took me a fucking hour just to put it together."

"Well, don't worry, buddy, the expert is here now," Mike boasted as he took off the jacket he was wearing over his T-shirt.

With the additional help, the job progressed quickly. By ten o'clock all the gear had been unpacked and assembled. The boys stepped back, admiring their handiwork. After a pause, they began cleaning up and moving all of the individual weights and dumbbells onto their respective racks. The sheer strenuousness of the job had gotten the two of them somewhat pumped up already.

"Okay, dude," John said as he grabbed Mike's upper arms from behind and kneaded them roughly, "it's time for the real workout. Let's try the bench first." He picked up a fifty-pound weight and slid it onto his end of the barbell.

Mike picked up another fifty-pounder and slid it onto the other end of the bar.

"You go first, I'll spot you."

"How can you do that?" Mike asked. "The back of the bench is right up against the wall. There's no place to stand."

"Hmm, you're right," John said with his hand to his chin. "How 'bout I just stand over from the front and spot you from there?"

"Sure, that'd be great," Mike said, despite the fact that it seemed kind of strange to him. Why didn't John want to move the whole contraption into the middle of the room? There was plenty of space.

Mike lay down and grasped the bar while John straddled the bench with his arms outstretched, and ready to offer assistance. Staring up at his muscular friend, Mike paused a second, affecting a look of concentration while really just stealing a good long look at John's tensed, beefy arms and the smooth, rounded chest hanging so deliciously close above him. He could see a few beads of moisture trapped in the hair beneath John's powerful arms. Mike was forced to pull his mind away from such things in order to keep his swelling cock from making itself obvious.

He took a deep breath and quickly raised the hundred pounds up over his chest. He pumped the weight up and down about twelve times in rapid succession. Then he returned the barbell to its resting place with a little assistance from John. Mike's quickened breathing was the only visible sign that he had expended any effort.

"Good job," John said as he grabbed two tenpounders and added one to each side of the barbell. "Let's see you try one twenty."

Mike stared at John's crotch, only about a foot away when, John had moved back into position. He could plainly see the outline of John's massive cock straining against the tight material of those ancient workout shorts. God! It almost looked like he wasn't wearing a jock-strap underneath it. In fact, as Mike breathed in deeply, he detected a powerful, musky, sweaty smell that must have been coming from John's balls. The smell and that thought were all that was necessary to trigger a raging hard-on in Mike's jeans. In a desperate attempt to divert his mind as quickly as possible, he hoisted the weights into the air and did his repetitions with as much intensity as he could muster.

"Intense, dude," John said as the weights came back to rest. "Now let me have a shot at it."

Mike stood up, twisting his body as best he could to turn the protrusion in the front of his jeans away from his friend. John set himself down on the bench and, looking Mike right in the eyes with his own steely blue gaze, the handsome, dark-haired young man said, "Now it's your turn to do me, buddy."

Mike was taken aback for a second by the intensity of John's stare, but he quickly got into the straddling position, hoping that John wouldn't see the hard-on through his jeans.

John did see it, though, and at that moment his hopes and suspicions about his best friend were confirmed. And now, he decided, would be as good a time as ever to do something about it.

"Shit, man," he said, "I should have given you some workout shorts. Your legs must be pretty cramped all packed up into those jeans."

As he said this, John brought his hand up and began to rub and massage Mike's thighs through the rough denim material. Mike just stood there in stunned disbelief as his hunky friend started to feel him up. John took the silence as encouragement and moved his hands toward Mike's bulging crotch. As John's fingers touched the throbbing mound, Mike let out a sigh and almost instinctively reached back to grab John's own rock-hard erection.

"Oh yeah, buddy; I've been waiting for this for so long," John whispered as he reached up and began to pull down Mike's zipper. Just then, John's father burst into the garage.

"Oh, John," he sobbed, "I hate to be the one to tell you."

He was so obviously distraught that he hadn't even noticed the signs of the heavy scene that was only just beginning to transpire. John nearly passed out, and Mike went white as a sheet.

"What is it, Dad?" John asked, visibly startled, but already figuring his father hadn't seen anything.

"It's your Great Aunt Hildegard. She's passed away in her sleep!"

John's first thought was: Who the hell is Aunt Hildegard? His second thought was: Why the fuck did she have to kick the bucket just as I was about to make it for the very first time with my super-hot-looking best friend? His third thought was: Screw the insulation, I'm getting my own apartment by Christmas if I have to hustle burgers at the neighborhood White Castle to do it.

"Oh, I'm sorry, Dad," he said, trying to sound solemn. "When's the funeral?"

"That's part of the reason I'm falling apart. It's tomorrow morning and it's an eight-hour drive from here. We have to get packed and on the road as quickly as possible!"

John's and Mike's hearts sank. They looked at each other with expressions of utter frustration on their faces. Mike quietly stood up, his penis now flaccid, and grabbed his sweater and coat. "I'm awfully sorry, Mr. Wallach. I guess I should get going."

"Yes, Mike. Thank you."

"Give me a call when you get back, okay, John?" Mike asked hopefully.

"You bet, buddy," John said, grabbing Mike's shoulder and squeezing it. "We'll continue just where we left off."

As Mike walked down the cool, dark street, he had a hard time convincing himself that the last fifteen minutes had actually taken place. But they had. He could tell by the pit of frustration in his stomach and the knot that had pulled tight in his balls. What had just happened was so amazing! There was someone else like him on the team—his best friend. He was making his own fantasies come true.

"Fuck!" was all he said.

He was just about ready to turn toward home when he remembered Kevin's invitation. Shit! He could stand to get stoned right about now. It sure beat going home at 10:30 on a Friday night, so he turned around and headed in the direction of Scott Gorseth's house.

CHAPTER THREE

III

Scott had lost his mother when he was only four, so he had ended up being raised primarily by his father. In the last few years, his father's success as a salesman had been increasing steadily, and Scott was finding himself alone in their big, spacious home more and more often.

Mike was familiar enough with Scott's place, and he automatically went around the house so that he could enter through the back patio. The Gorseths had one of the most incredible backyards in the entire town. A stream ran through a thicket of woods, far to the rear of their property. Along with the two huge fences that ran along both sides of their home, this gave them almost complete privacy.

As he approached the gate, Mike heard voices and laughter coming from the yard. He decided to take a peek through a space in the fence before barging in, and what he saw instantly caught his interest. Scott and Kevin were running back and forth in the yard tossing a football between the two of them. All they were wearing were running shorts, and Kevin, as he ran, had a glowing joint clenched in his teeth.

Mike got a much better view of his cousin's athletic body now than he had last week at the wrestling meet. Kevin's bare torso glistening in the moonlight sent chills down Mike's spine. Scott looked even better as he leaped in the air to catch the returned football. The dark-blond nineteen-year-old was always shy and quiet around most people, and Mike had never realized what an incredible body he was hiding. His stomach was especially impressive, rippling with well-defined muscle before disappearing into his baggy red running shorts.

Now Scott was chasing after Kevin, who had just taken possession of the ball. Flinging himself forward, he managed to grab him around the waist. Kevin's bare feet slipped on the wet grass and he came tumbling down with Scott on top of him.

What Mike saw next shot through him like lightning.

Scott and Kevin started to kiss. Wrapping their muscular arms around each other, the two of them squirmed in the damp grass and began to grind their hips together.

Mike watched with growing excitement as they made out right there on the lawn, oblivious to everything else. Kevin jabbed his tongue into Scott's mouth as his hands worked their way into his buddy's shorts to grab onto his firm ass. Just as he did, Scott rolled over, pulling Kevin on top of him. Then Kevin did likewise and they wrestled and rolled through the moonlit green.

When the horseplay stopped, they were both lying beside each other laughing at how the other one was covered with grass and grass stains. They also noticed that they each had a raging hard-on, and Scott leaned over Kevin's crotch and pulled back his running shorts and jock-strap. Kevin assisted him in getting them off and then lay back down in the grass. His six-inch cock stood up, straight and proud, saluting the star-spangled sky, while the fresh evening chill caused his nuts to draw up tightly.

Scott licked his lips and lowered his mouth to Kevin's erection. He started at the base of the cock and took a long lick all the way up to the purplish cap. Kevin shivered and brought his hands up behind his head. Scott then engulfed the top of Kevin's cock with his mouth. His tongue licked around the ridge of the head and wrapped itself around the stalk. Pulling back his tongue, he plunged down to the base as he deep-throated Kevin's shaft. He stayed there briefly, his nose in Kevin's pubic hair, inhaling the musky aroma. As he pulled his mouth up the length of the hard penis he closed his fist tightly around the base of it, creating a pressure that caused Kevin to moan and squeeze his eyes shut.

Kevin's fleshy bulb had enlarged perceptibly, and Scott continued sucking it feverishly. Jabbing his tongue into the piss-hole, Scott tasted a few drops of his best friend's pre-cum and swallowed it down greedily. Then moving away from the cock, he licked his way up Kevin's hairless torso, pausing briefly while he played and bit at the nipples. As Kevin wriggled with delight, Scott proceeded up past his neck until his mouth once again clamped down onto Kevin's.

While locked in the deep kiss, Kevin reached down and started to inch off the tightly packed pair of shorts and the bulging jock strap that Scott was still wearing. Realizing that Kevin couldn't get them off while they were locked in such a tight embrace, Scott let the kiss end and rose to his feet with Kevin still lying in the grass between his legs.

A shiver ran through Kevin and his cock stiffened even more as he looked up at his incredibly hot buddy. Scott Gorseth was one of those guys who seemed to have been born with a perfectly proportioned muscular body. Even when they were kids Mike could remember thinking that Scott had a studly bod for a younger guy. And it seemed that his perfect body had gotten even better since he began wrestling. Especially in the legs. Apparently, both Mike and Kevin had grown pretty hot for him. Mike thought Scott had the sexiest thighs he'd ever seen on anybody. Later, Mike would learn that Kevin liked to say Scott had the "thighs and ass of death."

From the passionate look in his pale green eyes, it was obvious that Scott was also pretty fond of Kevin. He ran both his hands through his short-cropped, dark blond hair while he tensed his muscles for Kevin's benefit. Lowering his hands to his waist, he proceeded to slip off his shorts and jock.

"God, you have a beautiful cock," Kevin said in a voice gravelly with lust.

"You know it's all yours, Kev. So why don't you come and get it?"

Kevin got up to kneel between Scott's legs. For a second, he just stared at the twitching piece of cock meat that stood raptly before him. It pointed perfectly straight into the air. All nine, thick inches of it. And even in the cool night air, the hefty balls hung low in their sac. Kevin's mouth came down on that gorgeous cock and furiously began to make love to it. His head pistoned up and down the length of Scott's dick, slicking it with his hot saliva. Soon, the motions became even quicker as Scott put his hands on

Kevin's head and started to use his powerful hips to thrust in and out of his buddy's mouth.

From his view crouched behind the fence, Mike watched in amazement as his viciously foxy "little cousin" deep-throated Scott's impressive cock.

After a few minutes of this heavy activity, Scott pulled his dick free. "Lie down on your back, Kev, before you make me shoot. I wanna get another taste of your cock."

The two muscular young men got into a sixty-nine down in the grass and, in a frenzy, began to work over each other's cocks. As Mike's own big prick was trying to rip its way through his jeans, he recalled that he had been invited to this party. Now looked like a good time to make his presence known. He opened the gate as quietly as he could, not that it made much difference. Scott and Kevin were so deep into their mutual blowjobs that an air attack could have gone on unnoticed. Oblivious to Mike's presence less than ten feet away, the roiling pair had clearly set sail beyond the point of no return.

Scott's gorgeous ass muscles flexed and unflexed as he drove his cock into and out of Kevin's sucking mouth. His own mouth was equally busy as it slid up and down on Kevin's upthrust dick. Scott's upper arms bulged as he held himself over his best friend's crotch. As Mike rubbed his own huge bulge through the denim of his jeans, Scott pulled his mouth off Kevin's twitching prick.

"Oh, fuck, man, I'm gonna come," he said. "It's just too fucking good."

Mike just about came himself as he beheld a look of sheer rapture come over Scott's handsome face. Scott shuddered and moaned as his swollen cock could finally take no more, and began to pump a massive load into Kevin's mouth.

It seemed that the taste of all that gushing cum was all that Kevin needed to reach his own climax, and just as a thin rivulet of Scott's juice had begun to seep out of the corner of his mouth, he bucked his hips and shot the first volley of his own ejaculation up into Scott's face.

Scott, realizing that he was AWOL, immediately clamped his mouth down on the geysering cock and succeeded in swallowing down the remainder of Kevin's sizable load.

Only as Scott rolled off from atop Kevin did he notice Mike standing there. Without even batting an eye he tapped Kevin on the shoulder to get him to look in Mike's direction.

"Hey, dude, how'd you like the show?" Scott asked with a mischievous glint in his eyes.

Kevin turned toward his cousin and said, "Far out! I was hoping you'd come by. Want a hit?" He got up and began rummaging around in the grass for the joint he had dropped earlier. It didn't take long for him to find the massive Bob Marley-sized bomber and relight it.

As he took the joint from Kevin, Mike marveled at what a couple of laid-back dudes these guys were. It had to have been the weed! After all, how many guys could there be in the world who, when caught by a friend or relative bare-assed and sucking on their buddy's dick, would nonchalantly offer them a hit on a joint? He took a deep puff.

"Fuck," Mike said as he sat himself down on the ground next to the two naked young men. "That was one of the hottest things I've ever seen in my life. I nearly came in my pants."

"Shit, it looks like you nearly ripped a hole in your jeans with that hard-on of yours," Scott said in an admiring tone.

"How long have you been screwing around together?" Mike asked as he took another long hit on the joint.

"Since about two weeks after I moved in with you guys," said Kevin. "I know your parents and my mom and dad wanted to keep this their 'dirty little secret,' but who the fuck cares what I do with my dick? It's my business. When Scott and me both started on the wrestling team, we would practice together, and one thing led to another."

"Yeah, but if we had known there were any other interested parties, we could have given ourselves a more varied workout," Scott said as he stared straight into Mike's blue eyes.

"I don't know, Scott," Kevin said with a grin, "we don't want to share our workout with someone whose body isn't up to a wrestler's standards. Have you ever seen how scrawny most gymnasts are? And look at that little beer gut he's gettin'."

"Fuck!" Mike drew out the word, grinning with gleeful mock-resentment as he rose to his feet and stuck his chest out.

"Hmm, you may be right," Scott said with a smirk on his face. "I think we're going to have to see some proof that you're in good enough condition before we let you participate in our extracurricular activities."

As it dawned on Mike what the two younger hunks were up to, he slowly slipped his jacket off his back. The two naked boys sitting in the grass were losing their cool demeanor as their cocks began to harden again. The reaction made Mike smile as he slipped off his sweater and then paused for a moment to flex his muscles, which were still pumped up enough by his earlier workout to push the fabric of his undershirt to its limits. Slowly he peeled off his white T-shirt, pausing for a moment so that the boys could admire the nearly flat, rippling surface of his stomach. He kicked off his tennis shoes and slowly brought up one foot at a time to remove his socks. When he finally pulled his shirt over his head, he left his forearms trapped by the material for a moment as he turned his back on his audience to display his powerful shoulders and thickening triceps.

With his T-shirt off, he turned back to Scott and Kevin and ran his hands through his hair in a deliberately slow, seductive movement. He stretched his performance out for this surprising pair of horny guys, who were already stroking their completely erect cocks.

"Oh, fuck, this is great," Scott said as his hand ran up and down on his cock. "I've wanted to see you naked for so fucking long."

This statement made Mike's own cock twitch, because he had lusted after the hunky wrestler quite a few times himself. He was determined not to rush his striptease, though, as he unbuttoned his jeans and methodically began to pull down the zipper. Mike's cock burst through as soon as his fly was completely undone, now restrained only by the thin elastic material of his jock-strap. Pushing the denim over the tree-trunk girth of his thighs, he finally let the jeans fall and stepped out of them.

Mike was silent, standing there in nothing but his jock-strap, his big dick twitching, wildly trying to get out. He slipped his fingertips into the waistband of his jock and slid them around, pulling at it where ever it bit into the soft flesh beneath his bellybutton and at his sides. Then he pushed the jock off in one quick movement.

Scott stared only for a moment at the stiff eight inches of meat and the light brown pubic hair that tapered up to a thin line at Mike's navel. He immediately stood up, moved over to Mike, placed his lips firmly onto the older man's chest and started licking at the quickly stiffening nipples.

Mike let out a long, passionate moan, as he began his very first sexual encounter with another man.

"All right!" was all Kevin had to say.

Scott worked his way slowly down Mike's chest and stomach as he lowered himself to his knees, kissing and licking at the firm, sculpted flesh, tasting the salty dried sweat on Mike's skin. When he reached a kneeling position, Scott found himself face to face with Mike's cock. He only looked for a second, though, before closing his eyes and lowering his mouth onto that hot, throbbing piece of manmeat.

"Oh, yeah," Mike moaned, as he closed his eyes and threw his head back. Scott's tongue wrapped itself around Mike's erection, tickling at the sensitive underside of the bulbous head. The sensation was so much more incredible than Mike could ever have believed, so much more real. Soft and warm, yet with an intense pressure that kept building and building, never allowing him to catch his breath. As Scott took the entire cock into his mouth, Mike whimpered uncontrollably as he reached down and ran his hands through the sexy teenager's short-cropped hair. He couldn't believe this was happening to him as he watched Scott bury his face in his pubic hair.

Mike was so caught up in his blowjob that he didn't even notice his cousin standing up and stepping around behind him. Kevin kneeled down to his older cousin's rear and pulled apart Mike's firm ass cheeks. When the puckered hole was exposed, he immediately jammed his tongue into it.

Mike let out a growl as a bolt of pleasure shot through him, the likes of which he had never felt before. Kevin jabbed his tongue in and out of the sensitive hole rapidly, each time causing Mike's cock to jerk in Scott's hot mouth. Scott had no problem with that, though, because each time it happened, a small burst of pre-cum was being deposited on his tongue. It tasted so good, in fact, that the horny nineteen-year-old grew determined to get the real thing as quickly as possible.

Increasing the pressure in his mouth as he sucked up and down, Scott proceeded to turn Mike's cock into a piece of polished granite, and Mike was very rapidly losing all sense of control. He practically screamed as Kevin stabbed his tongue into his asshole at the same time Scott clamped his mouth tightly around the base of his cock.

Mike's mind reeled. He felt as if he'd gone mad; as if he'd realized he was dreaming but had no way of ever waking up. An hour ago he was cut off—maybe forever—twelve inches away from realizing his lustiest fantasy. Ten minutes ago, no one had ever touched his dick other than himself, and a few overeager girls on pointless, shallow dates. But now, there he was, standing in the moonlight with his little cousin's tongue up his butt, and this hot and hunky young wrestler sliding his mouth up and down on his hard eight-inch cock.

Kevin was really getting off on the taste of his cousin's hot ass as he licked up and down the entire sweaty crack. Mike spread his legs farther apart to facilitate this amazing activity, allowing for Kevin to lick his way under to eventually reach his balls. Kevin bit lightly on the furry sac, causing Mike to let out a cry that couldn't be identified as either pleasure or pain, and he grabbed fiercely onto Scott's head, driving himself even harder into the wrestler's hungry mouth. Scott's tongue had become a blur. His hands grabbed onto the backs of Mike's thighs as he gave full priority to the superb blowjob he was delivering to his buddy's cousin.

Mike couldn't take it any longer. Just as Scott dive to the base of his cock, Kevin, once again, jabbed his tongue up his ass, this time pushing it clear through Mike's tight anal sphincter. Mike exploded in a gut-wrenching orgasm.

Scott mewed with pleasure as the hot, salty cum suddenly flooded his mouth and began to rush down the back of his throat. He succeeded in swallowing blast after blast of Mike's huge load. After one long, delirious moment, Mike slowly floated back to earth. When his eyes focused again, he saw his cousin standing in front of him, absently running his hands up and down his naked torso, and wearing nothing but a shit-eating grin on his face. Next to him was Scott, who was licking his lips and stroking his raging hard-on. It only took Mike a second to realize what he wanted to do.

Mike got down on his knees, looked up at Kevin, and smiled just before he lowered his mouth onto his cousin's dick.

"Yeah, Mike, suck my cock."

Mike loved the feel of Kevin's dick in his mouth. It was so meaty and alive. It pulsated between his tongue and the roof of his mouth, and he had to remember to relax his gullet as the throbbing rod proceeded toward his throat. The head was smooth and silky, while the stalk was ribbed with heavy veins. When his lips reached the base, he found a prickly tangle of pubic hair, and as he deep-throated his cousin, he pressed his nose into the hair and inhaled the musky scent.

After a few more licks, Mike came up for air. "Man, Kev. Your dick tastes great."

"You should try this one, then."

Mike's eyes almost crossed as he turned and found Scott's nine-inch beef pole staring him in the face. He momentarily lost his breath while trying to even imagine being able to take this giant of a cock. He was definitely game to try, though.

"Suck that cock, cuz!" Kevin encouraged as Mike took the fat head of Scott's dick into his mouth. Meanwhile, Kevin lazily stroked his own piece of meat, now well-slicked with his cousin's affection.

Mike grabbed onto the base of Scott's dick for support as he slowly worked his sweltering mouth down its length. For a brief instant, he had the entire cock in his mouth, but he began to gag and had to pull back up. Then he switched back to his cousin and worked on his dick for a couple of minutes; and then once again, it was back to Scott's.

Grabbing both dicks in his hands, he maneuvered the two wrestlers as close to one another as possible and valiantly tried to suck both cocks at once. He managed to get about halfway down the two stalks, but that was it. Appreciating every moment of Mike's attempts, the two studs locked a solid grip onto each other's upper arms for support as Mike went back to alternating between them. As usual with new things that caught his fancy, he was a fast learner and was quickly driving both of them toward a climax.

Scott began to thrust his cock up against Mike's face while it wasn't being sucked on, and soon Kevin was doing likewise. Mike enjoyed this cock-lashing almost as much as the blowjobs he was giving, and it was all he could do to keep from being overwhelmed by this incredible experience.

The constant friction on his dick was too much for Kevin; and the next time his cousin swallowed his cock, he sank his tensing fingers deeply into Mike's short hair, and held him down on his cock as he shot his load deep into his greedy mouth. Mike struggled mightily to keep from choking upon the salty fruit of his cousin's loins, savoring the taste of the ropy sperm as he let it linger on his tongue. The fact that it tasted just like his own gave him a cool sense of satisfaction.

Scott's hand flew up and down on his own dick as he watched his buddy shoot his load down Mike's throat. The sight was an incredible turn-on and helped push him closer toward his own climax. Mike saw the muscles in Scott's neck and shoulders tighten as he finished swallowing Kevin's cum, and he was pretty sure he knew what that meant. He immediately let go of Kevin's cock and clamped his mouth over Scott's tool just in time to catch the first volley of the hot wrestler's spurting orgasm.

Scott's sperm was even saltier-tasting than Kevin's, but still delicious in its own way. It kept coming and coming, and Mike wasn't sure if he could swallow it all, but he gave it his best shot. To his credit, only a trickle escaped, and when Scott lifted Mike to his feet, he licked it off as he gave Mike a deep, luscious kiss.

CHAPTER FOUR

IV

Mike lay in bed the next morning with a faint layer of perspiration on his body, and his thick, aching arms behind his head. Even though it was only October, his mother had the furnace cranking out heat like it was the middle of January.

He only had one sheet covering him, and it was pulled up just to his waist. He was completely nude, and his cock was outlined clearly under the thin fabric. He had lost his jock-strap somewhere in Scott Gorseth's yard last night. Reaching a hand down under the sheet, he fondled his rapidly hardening cock as he recalled the events of the previous evening. He still couldn't believe what had happened between him and his best buddy, John Wallach.

Fuck; to think that all this time Johnny-boy had been just as interested in his dick as he was in John's. Well, as soon as John got back, they'd be making up for some lost time.

And then there was Kevin and his buddy, Scott. Shit, they were a couple of hot little fuckers. Fuck! Little was hardly the word for them. His cousin's dick wasn't quite as big as his own, but it was big enough, and he still couldn't get over the impressive piece of meat that Scott had between his legs. They were sexy dudes. Between his thoughts of them and his thoughts of John, Mike found himself stroking a major hard-on.

He pulled the sheet away, exposing his rock-hard cock as he pulled himself up against the bed's back-board. Spreading his knees apart, he lavished full attention on his dick. He stroked it languidly as he thought of what he and John would do when John got back. He closed his eyes and imagined John's tautly muscled torso with beads of sweat clinging to his tanned skin. The two of them would just be standing there, face to face, totally naked, staring into each other's eyes. John had the darkest, sexiest eyes Mike could imagine, with thick, masculine eyebrows and delicate, long, almost feminine eyelashes. Their cocks would be rock hard and twitching slightly against each other in the midst of their trembling excitement.

Mike held the image in his head as his hand slid up and down the length of his stiff cock. God, he loved beating off! Even with John, Scott, and Kevin to fool around with now, he couldn't even imagine not sneaking off to be by himself occasionally, to play with his dick until it shot a load.

Every muscle in his body began to tighten, and he involuntarily found his body rising off the bed as he neared his climax. He moaned as he felt the sperm churning in his balls as he continued to pound on his cock. And then, with one final deep, throaty grunt, the undeniable release came as load after milky load shot onto the tight muscles of his chest and stomach.

As the last faint bursts dribbled from the flared head of his prick, Mike reached for the towel beside his bed and used it to wipe the sticky mixture from his torso.

When he was done, he jumped out of bed, wrapped the soiled towel around his waist, and headed for the shower. His still-partially-erect dick showed plainly through the tightly wrapped towel as he walked down the hallway. When he made it to the bathroom safely, he pulled the towel off, letting his dick flop free, and tossed it down the laundry chute. It never dawned on him that his mother knew exactly what was going on every time she pulled one of those sticky towels out of the hamper in the basement. Between him and his houseguest cousin, she'd seen plenty of them.

After a quick shower, Mike went back to his room and pulled on a fresh jock-strap, running shorts, and a tank top. Over all that, he pulled on a pair of red sweatpants and a hooded sweatshirt, and he finished off his day's wardrobe with sweatsocks and running shoes.

"So I'm gettin' a slight beer gut, huh?" he murmured to himself in his mirror, as he pulled his sweatshirt tight around his torso and gave his stomach a few probing jabs. Only the slightest hint of softness was noticeable through the fabric. His appraising eyes caught the barest swell of baby fat over the muscles of his belly, and he could still pinch the last vestiges of those off-season love handles that had sneaked around his sides; nothing more. Still, it was noticeable enough for Scott and Kev to tease him. "Well, we'll see about that!"

Finally, he went downstairs and into the kitchen, where his parents would see him post-blowjob for the first time.

Richard and Marge were sitting at the table reading the newspaper, dad sipping coffee and silently nursing a hangover.

"Hi, Mom. Hi, Dad. Has Kevin gotten home yet?"

"No," said Marge, "he called and said he was going to spend the day over at Scott's."

Mike laughed to himself as he thought about what those two horny fuckers would be up to all day.

After downing a quick glass of milk and a couple of raw eggs, he headed for the door. "I'm going out to run a few miles. I'll be back in a couple of hours."

"That's nice, honey," his mother said without looking up as he slipped out the door.

Mike made his way to the old airport road a few miles south of town. It was a lonely stretch of highway about three klicks long that used to bring shorthop commuters to the county's rusting municipal airport. The airport had been torn down about five years ago when funding came through for the completion of a brand new state-of-the-art airport on the other side of town, and all that was left now was a deserted stretch of pavement that nobody ever used. Even weekend dragsters had abandoned the road after the local sheriff's department placed highway patrolmen out there on the odd Saturday night.

Of course, that's what Mike loved about this piece of road. As he ran down the center line, he felt like he was the only person in the world. This blue highway was all his and he could do whatever he wanted here. His Saturday morning runs were special, and almost nothing could keep him from them. It was his chance to really cut loose; to feel the potential of his body as the miles pounded beneath his feet. It all felt so physical, so powerful, so fucking wonderful.

As he neared completion of his first mile, he began to really sweat. Even though it was a cool, early-October morning, the sun was beating directly down on him and he was getting uncomfortably hot. Without slowing his pace even a little, Mike pulled off his hooded sweatshirt and tossed it to the side of the road as he continued to run.

The sweat was visibly running down his broad shoulders, soaking into the thin, ribbed material of his muscle shirt. The sudden feel of the cool air gave him a burst of energy, and Mike ran faster. It would only take another minute of running before he stopped noticing the temperature, and the sweat on his shoulders and chest was only beading now, evaporating in the cool air.

As he approached the end of his second mile, he slowed down to a jog as he loosened the drawstring around his waist. With a few quick steps, he had his legs free of the sweatpants and was tossing them to the side as well before returning to full speed. He could feel the strain of exhaustion beginning to creep into his legs. His powerful thighs and calves bulged and relaxed with every stride he took. The hair on his legs was matted down with sweat, and his socks grew damp over his lower legs, where the hair grew much thicker. As he pushed himself harder, the silky black material of his tight running shorts began to creep up the crack of his ass, exposing the leg straps of his jock and the lower portion of his hard, powerful leg muscles.

Now the sun was beating fully on him as he moved to within half a mile of his goal. His exertion forced sweat once again to stream freely from his body. With one quick motion, he slipped off the muscle shirt and tossed it behind him. For the last half mile, he was nothing but mindless physicality. His muscles were pumping like engines, and perspiration washed down his torso.

As the road curved around a thicket of trees to its completion at the old airport field, Mike was suddenly jolted back into reality and came to a complete stop. Sitting at the end of his racetrack was a parked van. Its back doors were open, and someone was sitting there watching him as he closed in on the finishing line.

At first, Mike was furious. Who would have the nerve to invade his running track? Soon enough, though, he caught his breath and calmed down a little. This was hardly private property. Besides, there was something awfully familiar about that van, and even more awfully cute about its owner.

Jason Carmichael got up to give Mike a lonely ovation for crossing the invisible finish line. What would the golden, rich dude be doing out here on a Saturday morning?

"Hey, buddy, how's it going?" Jason called to Mike as he made his final approach.

"I'm doing fine, man. What are you doing out here?"

"I just came out to think. I do that once in a while, you know—think?" He grinned. "But fuck, dude, you gotta be just about freezing to death."

It suddenly dawned on Mike that he was pretty cold. With no more exertion, the sweat on his body had dried, and now he found himself half-naked in the cool October air.

"Climb in and I'll shut the doors."

Mike did so, and Jason locked out the cold behind them. Typical of his rich-boy status, Jason's van was luxuriously furnished with plush carpeting, big comfortable pillows, and a refrigerator. Mike leaned back against a stack of cushions and scanned his surroundings. Jason sat down opposite him and pulled an envelope from behind the driver's seat.

"Here, dude, this'll warm you up," he said as he pulled out a joint and lit it. He took a deep toke and then passed it over to Mike, who accepted it gratefully and took a long, slow hit. As one would expect from Jason, the dope was first rate.

As he passed it back, Jason reached into the refrigerator and pulled out two cans of Budweiser. He took the joint and held it between his teeth as he opened one of the beers and handed it to Mike.

Still stinging from Kev and Scott's beer-gut jab last night, Mike considered not accepting the Bud, but then thought better of it. "Thanks. Nice custom job."

"You think so, man?" Jason said as he took a swallow and handed the joint back to Mike.

"Yeah." Mike took another drag. "I'm just trying to imagine all the wild things you could do with a set of wheels like this."

"You name 'em, buddy, and I've probably done them."

"Really," said Mike, grinning, his still-thumping heart racing the THC throughout his system. The wild stuff Jason was referring to couldn't possibly come close to what he was thinking.

"Yeah, man, I mean really kinky stuff!"

Within a few short moments, Mike realized he was getting really stoned. The beer and the grass had loosened him up, and now he was sitting there, half-naked across from the best-looking senior on the gymnastics squad as he talked about sex. He started to get a hard-on.

"What kind of kinky stuff, man?" Mike said half suspiciously, so as not to sound too eager.

Jason looked squarely into Mike's sexy blue eyes and slowly licked his lips. "You ever suck on another guy's dick?"

Mike's cock went totally hard. This guy wants me.

He fuckin' wants me! "N-no, man," he lied. "Have you?"

"Yeah, a few times," Jason said with a mischievous look in his eyes and a shit-eating grin on his face. "Judging from the hard-on in your shorts, I'd say you've thought about it a few times yourself."

Mike looked down at how obviously his cock was making a tent in his shorts, and then looked back up at Jason. By this point, he'd determined that Jason was seriously interested in him. He could see the huge piece of meat snaking down the leg of Jason's sweatpants, and it looked hard!

He coyly looked back at Jason. "I'll suck yours if you'll suck mine."

Jason started laughing. "Far out, dude," he said, and without further delay, he leaned over and pulled back Mike's tightly packed shorts and jock-strap and slid them down Mike's furry, hard, muscular legs. Jason began stroking his rock-hard piece of meat as he looked at Mike's entire naked body. It was clear he admired it. "You've got a hot-looking dick," he said in a husky whisper.

"Thanks," Mike half moaned as he closed his eyes and began to thrust his groin up and down into Jason's talented hands.

"In fact, your whole body is pretty fucking hot. I think it's time for me to have a taste of it."

"Go for it, dude."

Jason, still fully clothed, held himself over Mike's reclining body by his powerful arms and then slowly lowered his mouth to Mike's chest. He began kissing the space between Mike's large pectoral muscles, licking up the sweat that had dried there. From there, he moved slowly from one nipple to the other, sucking on each of them, playing with them with his tongue, and lightly biting on the little rock-hard nubs with his teeth. Mike had never had this done to his tits before, and it was making him harder than he ever remembered being.

After giving a last lick to the nipples, Jason chewed his way down Mike's firm abdomen, nibbling and tasting the lightly salted flesh. The flavor got him hungry for more, and he moved lower down Mike's belly, digging his teeth into the hard, rippling muscles that lay partially obscured beneath that last, slight layer of baby fat. Approaching the gently puckered meat around Mike's navel, Jason was delighted to discover the faint trace of hair that started there and quickly expanded to become thicker, as he munched his way closer to Mike's throbbing penis.

It was definitely getting hot in the close quarters of the van, so before continuing, Jason leaned back on his haunches, and, after freeing his T-shirt from the waistband of his sweats, pulled it off in one quick motion. Mike, who was half gone with lust, just stared up at the hot-looking senior.

Jason's body was not quite as husky as Mike's but possessed much finer definition. The hair under his arms was a bit darker than the short, dirty-blond hair on his head, but that was about all Mike had time to notice before Jason dived down and engulfed his dripping cock with his flesh-hungry mouth.

Mike moaned with pleasure as he watched the mouth of the guy every girl in his school lusted after slide up and down on his dick. He leaned back in the pillows with his arms behind his head and enjoyed the incredible blowjob he was receiving. God, this was too good to be true, he thought. Maybe he'd picked up a scent last night—a hot pheromone that made the men of his dreams starve for his thick meat. Or maybe, he mused, he simply had what it took to get guys like Wonder Bread super-jock Carmichael to bend a little and give it up. Who knew? And who cared!

Jason took Mike's entire cock in his mouth and plunged his head up and down its entire length a couple of times. He'd stop for a while with just the head in his mouth so that he could taste whatever pre-cum he had worked to the surface, and then he would repeat the whole process again and again. It seemed to be having the desired effect. Mike was so close to coming that his stiff cock was practically drooling now.

"Stop it, man. I don't want to blow yet."

Jason let the spit-soaked cock slip out of his mouth and leaned back on his haunches again. Perspiration trickled down the valley between his chest muscles. Raising himself to a kneeling position, he smiled sweetly as Mike, driven by sheer, over-whelming lust, crawled toward him. Sliding his hands around Jason's athlete's body, Mike kissed him full on the lips. Their tongues, dried by the pot smoke, playfully touched and slipped over one another. He took a firm hold of Jason's waist, dropped his head into his lap, and began to gnaw at the drawstring of his sweats with his teeth.

"Fuck, man," Jason said as he took this all in, "you can't wait to suck my cock, can you?"

Mike was silent as he undid the sweats and started to pull them down. The first thing he saw was Jason's thick bush of pubic hair. Jason wasn't wearing any underwear. Then came Jason's monster dick. It was at least the ten inches in length Mike had imagined it to be; and, right now, it was definitely all hard. He stifled a stoned giggle: how do these horse-hung studs stay conscious when so much blood rushes out of their skulls and into their nearly foot-long dongs!

"Go ahead, suck on it," Jason coaxed, apparently wide awake.

Mike needed no further encouragement. He lowered his mouth onto the flaring head of Jason's cock, and immediately tried to take the whole thing in his mouth, but started choking at the halfway point.

"Easy, man, you're not a sword swallower, yet," laughed Carmichael.

Mike pulled up and instead gave his full attention to the fat head. He snaked his tongue around it, feeling the ridge where it met the stalk. Jason's piss-hole had begun to flare, and Mike playfully jabbed his tongue into it.

"Fuck, man, you sure suck cock great!" Jason moaned. "Are you sure you haven't done this before?"

Mike just smiled as he gave one last lick to the head of Jason's dick and then turned his attention to the furry balls hanging below.

"Oh, yeah, suck on my nuts!"

Mike licked at them until the hair was soaked and matted. Then he turned to lie on his back, nodding and pushing his face up under Jason's balls as he licked his way toward the crack of his teammate's ass. Before last night, he never would have believed he'd be doing something like this; it just had never occurred to him in all his fantasies. How simple they had been! But that ass bath Kevin gave him last night had felt so incredible! The sheer variety of things that was possible made his heart triphammer. Jason softly moaned, as if in agreement. Gurgling, whispering unintelligible words, he then leaned over and began sucking madly on Mike's dick.

As Mike's tongue neared Jason's tight asshole, the musky smell drove him into an even higher state of frenzy, giving him no choice but to push himself through yet another dare. He used his fingers to pry the muscle open and darted his tongue inside.

Gasping, wriggling, Jason simply went nuts, and he pulled his mouth from Mike's cock. "Oh, God, that's great! Now stick your cock in. I gotta have you fuck me."

Mike was taken aback for a second. He had stuck his own finger up his ass lots of times; other things as well on occasion: pencil erasers, cleaned carrots, one of his father's plastic cigar casings. But quite honestly, it had never occurred to him that one day he might have a whopper of a cock knocking at his back door. Butt-fucking or getting rammed had not been a part of Mike's fantasy life; but then again, here was Jason Carmichael begging him to deliver it up his chute. The thought made his cock twitch, and with only those few seconds of hesitation he pulled himself out from beneath Jason.

Jason just stayed there on his hands and knees with his ass pointed in the air, "Yeah, Mike, stick your hot cock up my ass!"

Mike stroked his dick a few times. It was still wet from the blowjob Jason had been giving him. What the hell, he thought. The rich dude really does want me on top. Let him have me on top!

He held the tip up against Jason's tight hole and, after pressing against it a bit, slowly began to slide it in. He was amazed at how easily the muscle gave way, as the fat head of his cock pushed through the threshold of the sphincter.

"Oh, yeah, Mike," sighed Jason. "Slide it all the way in."

Mike did so until his pubic hair was pressed close to Jason's ass crack, and then simply held it there, allowing himself to indulge in the silky tightness of Jason Carmichael's ass. What an incredible feeling! It was as if his big cock were being grabbed and roughly squeezed by a soft, wet, muscular hand. Jason's ass seemed to be sucking Mike up by his dick all by itself. It would have been scary if it hadn't felt so damned good.

"Fuck me! Fuck me hard!"

Pulling out, then pushing back in, increasing the speed with each thrust, Mike looked down at Jason, who was moaning crazily now, sweat running down his muscular back. Their perspiration washed and mixed where Mike's lower belly wetly slapped against Jason's firm butt cheeks, raising a pungent, masculine smell out of their union. Leaning his chest against Jason's back, tenderly biting the nape of his neck, Mike reached his arms around to grab onto his teammate's nipples and raging hard-on. Nipples were pinched and cocks were teased and pulled upon, until the pair could barely take it any longer. Both college studs lost all sense of reality as their sweaty bodies pounded against one another and they both neared their points of no return.

Mike shot first, unloading what felt like gallons of hot cum inside Jason's tight ass. When he felt the searing heat washing into his bowels, Jason shuddered and called out, making a valiant effort to steady himself before shooting his own great wad. Mike felt it just as it started to erupt and he increased the speed and pressure of his strokes on Jason's cock. Carmichael shot three powerful blasts of sperm onto the carpeted floor of the van before finally turning his head to face Mike. A brief kiss to Mike's lips broke the spell, and then they both began to laugh.

As they stopped and picked up Mike's clothes on the drive into town, all Mike could think to himself was that Jason Carmichael had thought enough to kiss him when they were done.

CHAPTER FIVE

V

John Wallach couldn't fucking believe it. Twelve hours ago he was about to get into his best friend's pants, something he had dreamed about for years, and now here he was, some four hundred miles away, sitting at a funeral for some old bat he had never heard of before.

He had slept in the car for most of the drive down, but as the priest droned on in his monotone, he found himself drifting off from time to time until his mother elbowed him back to reality. He was sure that the only reason his parents could keep awake, despite driving so long, was that they were busy adding up in their heads just how much they stood to inherit off "poor" old Aunt Hildegard.

To help keep himself conscious for the rest of the service, he tried to imagine what he and Mike would do when he got back. It worked, but he ended up with a massive hard-on all through the rest of the mass. He quickly rearranged the hard piece of meat in his pants when he got up to exit the church, but it still flopped forward, making a tent in his dress pants. He hoped no one would notice, and he shoved his hands into his pockets to hide the effect.

Outside, they watched as the casket was loaded onto the hearse. John noticed that one of the pall-bearers wasn't much older than himself and was awfully cute to boot. He didn't have long to look, though, before everyone began climbing into cars to head out for the cemetery.

"So, Dad," John said as the got into their car, "how long before we can head back home?"

"Well, it looks like the reading of the will is going to be on Tuesday morning. We should be able to leave right afterward."

John's heart sank. "Dad, I really can't miss two days of classes and gym practice."

"I'm sorry, John, but it's unavoidable."

John was silent for the rest of the ride. Oh well, he thought, he'd just have to make up for it when he got back. The wicked thought brought a smile to his face just as they pulled into the cemetery.

When they got to the burial site, the casket was already in place and people were gathering around it. John looked around at the faces in the crowd and was amazed at how unattractive most of the people were. He hoped that the majority of them weren't related to him. Then he noticed the hunky pallbearer who had caught his eye outside of the church. Catching glimpses of him out of the corner of his eye, he found his interest becoming piqued. The guy had a strong, angular profile, boasting a pronounced jaw and a head of wavy black hair. He looked to be about twenty-one years old, stood six feet tall and looked pretty solidly built, but it was hard to tell with the navy blue suit that he was wearing. He certainly warranted further investigation, thought John lasciviously. In fact, John was so busy studying the guy that it caught him completely unaware when the handsome stranger turned and looked him square in the eyes, flashing him a discreet smile. Instantly flustered, John shyly turned away.

After the graveside ceremony, everybody piled back into their cars and headed back into town for a buffet lunch. The food looked pretty miserable so John opted for just a couple of sandwiches and a can of Pepsi. Sitting down at a table, he noticed his mother fortuitously speaking with Mr. Hot Pallbearer, and after a five-minute conversation, they both walked over to where he was seated.

"John," his mother said, "I'd like you to meet Lydia's nephew, Mark Simpson."

John was a bit dazed at having his secret little cruiser scenario so brilliantly fulfilled by his own mother, but he quickly composed himself and stood up to shake hands.

"Mark is a junior at the University of Minnesota, and he'll be leaving this afternoon to go back there. He says it would be no problem at all to drop you off at home on the way there."

"Yeah," Mark said, "it's not out of the way at all, and your mom tells me how anxious you are to get back." He gave John a big grin that showed off his perfect set of teeth, as well as the dimples in his cheeks.

"That's great," John said, doubly interested and brightening up considerably. "What time are you leaving?"

"I'll swing by your motel at about four. Can you be ready?"

"No problem, man. I'll be ready," John said with a laugh.

At four on the button, Mark pulled up in front of the Wallachs' motel in a black Jeep Wrangler that looked to be about a year old. He jumped out, threw John a hardy handshake, and opened the back door for John's stuff. He had changed into a pair of reasonably tight jeans and a T-shirt, and John was able to see now what had been hidden earlier by that bothersome suit jacket of his.

Mark had muscular arms that stretched the cotton material of his T-shirt taut around his biceps, and he sported an equally developed chest. John could see his nipples faintly outlined through the fabric. Mark's narrow waist only helped to highlight the rest of his torso.

"I don't know about you, man, but I don't think I could have taken one more minute with this stale group of relatives," said Mark as he gunned the engine.

John started laughing and immediately warmed to this hunky relative-out-of-nowhere of his. Maybe his luck had turned.

"So, I hear you do a lot of gymnastics in college."

"Yeah, I have for a couple of years," John answered.

"It seems to have done wonders. You're in pretty good shape."

John's body tingled a little bit. "Thanks, man, looks like you work pretty hard on yourself, too. Do you do gymnastics?"

"Nah, this is all from free weights, lots of heavy reps."

"Well, it seems to have done the trick."

"Thanks."

"Do you live in a dorm at the University?"

"No. I did my freshman year, but then me and two of my buddies rented a house just off of campus."

"That's got to be great being on your own like that; having all that freedom."

"Yeah, it's nice. I can do things I never could have done at home. Being in a city helps, too. Anything you want to find is there someplace."

John and Mark kept up the small talk for about four hours until it started to get dark and they began to get hungry. They decided to grab a bite and pulled into a truck stop somewhere in southern Iowa. It didn't seem to take long before they both polished off truck-driver-sized meals, and John marveled at Mark's musculature as he stretched his arms out and yawned.

"I don't know about you, but I'm kind of tired." Mark was scratching his left pec through his T-shirt. "I drove all the way down here last night with hardly any sleep, and I'm not sure I can handle it again so soon."

John affected a reasonably legitimate yawn and nodded agreement.

Mark grinned. "How about if we spend the night at that motel across the street and then we'll take off first thing tomorrow?"

"Sounds good to me," John replied, already considering the possibilities.

They paid for their meals and then hopped into the Jeep for the quick ride across the highway to the motel. John waited outside while Mark went in to get a room, and after about ten minutes he returned with a key and something in a paper bag.

"They're booked pretty full, and all that was left was a single. I hope you won't mind sharing a bed."

"No problem," John thought about good old Mike

back home and decided that he wouldn't mind at all. Things hadn't even gotten started with Mike, and after all, he was getting to be a sort of undercover pro at this sort of thing, so to speak.

The room was small and stuffy, but it would do for the evening. They both threw their overnight bags onto the queen-sized bed, and then Mark pulled a six-pack of beer out of the bag he had brought with him from the lobby.

"All right!" John said with a big grin on his face. "Brewski!"

"I figured this wouldn't go to waste if I bought it," Mark said as he tossed John an ice cold can.

"So where do you go to college?" Mark asked after taking a chair and a few long gulps.

"Oh, I go to Edison Community College near St. Paul," said John, for the first time a little ashamed he hadn't shot higher in the university department. "I guess you could say it's sort of a glorified high school extension, but it's got a killer gym squad."

"You should think about moving on to the University of Minnesota to finish your B.A. It's really got a lot to offer."

"Really? Like what?"

"Well, for one thing, it's got a great gymnastics program. One of my roommates is on the squad. The college offers practically any educational program you could possibly think of as well." Mark paused, took a long drink, and then took the plunge. "I think the best thing, though, is that it's so big that just about any group you could possibly want to get in with exists there."

"Like what kind of groups?"

"Oh, anything, really." Mark shrugged. "There's a group for chess players, a theater group, there's agricultural groups, there's a gay group...." Mark finished his beer, and as he crushed the can, he looked John in the eye.

John took a deep drink of his beer. "Have you ever been to the gay group?" he asked as he returned the stare.

"A couple of times," Mark replied.

John continued to stare into the gorgeous pall-bearer's intense, steel-blue eyes until Mark rose and came over to John's chair.

"Stand up."

John did, never breaking eye contact.

"You're a hot little fucker, do you know that?" Mark breathed in a deep, husky voice as he grabbed John by his thick, muscular arms and kissed him hard on the lips.

John kissed back with equal intensity, opening his mouth to let in Mark's probing tongue. He'd never kissed anyone like this before, and the sensation was getting him more excited than he ever remembered being. As his tongue jabbed into Mark's hot mouth, John's hands ran up and down his cousin's hot, hard body, feeling his muscular back and his firm, rounded ass.

Mark was equally impressed with John. He'd usually made it with older guys, and never one with such a great body. They ground their stirring mounds together, growing bigger and hotter with each passing moment.

John was in heaven. He'd missed having such close contact with another hard body, and doing it this way instead of at some anonymous bar was better than he had ever imagined it would be. He couldn't get enough of it. For his part, Mark was amazed at the apparent size of his new buddy's equipment. The shaft pressing against his own through two layers of denim had to be at least eight inches long. The older man finally broke the kiss.

"God, you're hot!" he gasped.

"You too, dude," John panted huskily as he caught his breath. "I'm glad you offered me a ride."

"Yeah, me too, guy. Why don't you take off that shirt?"

John pulled it over his head, mussing his hair in the process. Mark stared admiringly for a moment at his temporary bunkmate's well-built, hairless torso before leaning down to start sucking on one of his small, stiff nipples.

John moaned as the stubble on Mark's chin scraped against his sensitive flesh. Mark licked up and down the crevice between John's pectoral muscles, and then he slowly, deliberately raised one of John's arms before diving, tongue-first, into the exposed armpit. He licked through the damp patch of hair and deeply inhaled the musky scent.

"Take your clothes off," John whispered urgently.

Mark stood back and stepped out of his shoes. He pulled his T-shirt off and tossed it aside, then unbuttoned his jeans and slid them off. His hard-on stretched out and off to the side beneath his jockey shorts, and he smiled as he watched John gawk at it with a sparkling lust in his eyes.

"Take off your pants, dude," Mark said as he slipped off his own underwear.

Without taking his eyes off Mark's hard cock, John unzipped his jeans and slipped them and his underwear off at the same time. The two stood in front of each other, both now completely naked. They couldn't help mentally comparing themselves. Both were extraordinarily well built, and though Mark's hair was longer and wavier, they were both dark. Mark's body was at peak condition, rugged, big, ripped and cut, whereas John's body was smooth and more traditionally sculpted; he had yet to finish working off all the fun-fat he'd put on during last summer's beer blasts with Mike and the team. His body was virtually hairless except for the tufts under his arms, the thick patch around his dick, and a light sprinkling on his legs. Mark, on the other hand, had hairier legs and a fine spread of hair on his chest that funnelled into a dark trail leading down to his crotch. Their cocks were evenly matched at about eight inches, but while John's hard dick curved and hung down, Mark's stood up straight and hard like an arrow.

The two of them stood face to face again and began to kiss as their dicks throbbed and twitched against one another. Never breaking their deep french kiss, Mark led John over to the bed and they eased themselves down upon it. Mark kissed his way down John's smooth, firm torso until he reached the hard piece of meat at his crotch. He took a few long licks at the underside as John began to moan, and then engulfed it whole with his hot mouth. Mark then swung himself around, never letting John's dick out of his mouth, until his own dick hung temptingly over John's face. Softly groaning, John salivated as he stared at the hot, hard cock that hung over him. It only took a moment for him to wrap his mouth around it. He loved the smell of his this dude's crotch and immediately swallowed the cock whole in order to bury his nose in Mark's pubic hair.

At the same time, Mark continued sucking on John's blood-engorged staff. He loved the curve in it, and he had never blown someone who leaked as much pre-cum before. It was almost a steady stream, and he loved the taste of the bittersweet spunk. In fact, he could tell by the amount of pre-cum, as well as the tightening in his balls, that John was about to shoot, so he quickened the nodding motions he made with his head, all but capturing the entire cock in his throat.

John could take it no longer. A white-hot load of creamy jism exploded into Mark's gullet. John simply had to let go of Mark's big dick to unleash a series of growling moans, and he closed his eyes as his distant relative finished sucking up the last of his orgasm.

Swallowing the last of John's cum, Mark turned around and straddled the older stud's beefy torso. John stared up at the hard cock now pointing up straight over his face.

"That was great, man!" he said, a post-orgasmic daze covering his face.

"Glad you liked it, dude, but we're not done yet." Mark grinned. "This night's just begun."

"Far out," said John. "I think this little whopper should be next up on the menu."

"You know it, dude. Say, my friend, have you ever taken a long, hard cock up your ass?"

"N-no," said John, his big eyes blinking innocently up at his fresh, humpy lover. "Doesn't it hurt?"

"A little, at first." Mark grinned, poking John in the belly and not believing a word. "But I think you'll realize a little pain is worth a little gain."

John still looked uncertain. He was plenty experienced as a top, but he'd never really let anyone up into his back door, and Mark's dick looked huge from this angle.

"Here, I have something that'll help," Mark said as he pulled a little bottle from his overnight bag.

"What's that?" John asked.

"Poppers," Mark replied. "You just take a sniff and you won't even think about any pain."

"Really?" John asked. "Is it like a drug?"

"Not really. Just take a whiff."

John hesitantly unscrewed the cap and took a brief sniff.

"Quick, put the lid back on!" said Mark.

John lay back as he felt the poppers take effect. First he felt like his head was expanding. He could feel his blood rushing, but then, just as quickly, everything went back to normal. "That seemed harmless."

"It is," said Mark. "So, will you let me fuck you?"

The idea was starting to turn John on, and his cock began to harden again, "Sure."

"Great!" Mark beamed. "Get on your knees. We'll do it doggy style."

John turned and kneeled and Mark spread his ass cheeks apart. "First I better slick you up a little."

John went completely hard as his obviously more experienced buddy stuck his tongue up his butt and began to rim his ass. As Mark did this, John grabbed the poppers and took another hit. This time, however, he was overwhelmed by an entirely different sensation. His cock felt harder than it had ever felt before, and he felt a need he had never known before.

"Oh, God," he moaned. "Man, I want you to fuck me! Fuck me with your hard fucking cock!"

"Get my dick wet first," ordered Mark, as he withdrew his tongue, turned around, and allowed John to attack his dick. John's mouth slid up and down on the shaft, soaking it with his saliva.

"That's good, man," Mark said as he grabbed one of John's muscular arms. "Why don't you try to sit on my dick instead."

John said nothing as he rose and squatted over the athlete's towering piece of meat. Mark held his shaft steady as he guided John's ass down onto it. Seconds later, John screamed as the cock pierced his asshole. Suddenly, the effects of the poppers were gone.

"Oh fuck, it hurts!"

"Easy, man," Mark soothed. "Take it slowly. Here, why don't you take another hit."

John took the bottle and inhaled. He handed it back to Mark, who did likewise. In another minute or two, the pain subsided and he began to sink farther onto the shaft. When it was completely in, he felt a warm, voluptuous rush hit him again. His thick, muscular thighs tensed as he started to raise himself off Mark's thick eight inches, and then they relaxed again as he slammed himself back down upon it. A feeling of intense sexual pleasure was now washing over him, and his mind became oblivious to anything else. He looked down at his hot, hunky bunkmate as he raised and lowered himself on the throbbing shaft and took pleasurable note that Mark was equally far gone; his eyes were glazing over as he looked up at this hot, sweaty, sexy gymnast sliding up and down on his bursting dick.

Short of Mike, Mark looked like the sexiest person John had ever seen. He became lost in his sexual frenzy as he looked down at Mark's muscular torso. He couldn't slam himself down hard enough on that burning hot prick, and he could swear he heard his own heart beating and the blood rushing to his rock-hard cock as he rode on. His muscular left arm tensed as he shifted his body's weight to it and began to jack on his dick with his free right hand. Before long, his face turned red and his eyes clenched shut as he jammed himself down on Mark's cock and held himself there for a single, golden moment. Then his dick erupted in the most gut-wrenching, mind-blowing orgasm that he had ever experienced. A fountain of searing cum shot into the air and onto Mark's muscular chest. A few drops even reached his chin, landing there to glisten just under his soft, parted lips, only to be greedily lapped up by his hungry tongue.

The taste of John's cum knocked the delirious college jock over the edge, and he let loose a screaming, steaming volley of his own jism deep into his buddy's muscular ass.

John sat there looking dazed for a few minutes as Mark's cum ran out of his ass, and then he leaned over and kissed his hunky bedbrother on the lips, licking up his own sperm in the process.

The night turned into one long, sexual escapade as Mark showed John every possible position, including a few only a true gymnast could pull off. When they finally fell asleep in each other's arms at about four in the morning, they had both come five times each.

The next morning, they took off around eleven, and by the middle of the afternoon, Mark dropped John off at home. During the trip, John told Mark all about Mike, and Mark invited both of them to meet his two roommates when they were in Minneapolis the next weekend for the state tournaments.

"Thanks for the ride, man," John said as he jumped out of the Jeep. All he could think of, though, as he stepped away, was that he had the house to himself for the next twenty-four hours.

CHAPTER SIX

VI

The Belsons were just finishing dinner when the phone rang. Marge answered it as she was getting up to clear the table. "Hello, Belson residence. Oh, hello, John." Her voice always got just a bit warmer when it was John on the phone. "Yes, I'll get him. By the way, I'm so sorry about your aunt."

When Mike heard who it was, he practically knocked the table over in his hurry to get to the phone. "Hey, dude, how'd you get home so soon?"

"I'll have to tell you about that later. How would you like to come over and finish that workout we started the other night?"

"Man, you know I want to." Mike's voice was nice and smooth, but he was actually damned relieved. It had been so long, he almost started thinking maybe he'd imagined their little close encounter in the garage.

"I was hoping so. By the way, my parents are still

way outta town, and they're gonna stay that way for a little while."

"No shit!" The implications boggled Mike's mind.

"No shit, dude, so you'll be staying overnight, is that right?"

"I think that can be arranged." Mike wanted to scream, but he kept his cool in front of his snooping mother.

"One more thing, dude. Don't bother bringing pajamas."

"You can count on it."

Mike was a bundle of contained ecstasy as he hung up the phone. He told his parents he'd be spending the night at John's, and Kevin just gave him a shit-eating grin. As he opened the back door, Mike grinned back to confirm his cousin's every horny suspicion.

He practically ran the half mile to John's, but he was barely out of breath as he rang the Wallachs' doorbell. That kind of run would have winded him this time last year; he was improving, and things had never been better. With that romp in Jason Carmichael's van the other day, in fact, he figured he'd be ready for anything.

John answered the door wearing only a tank top and a pair of running shorts so tight that Mike could plainly see his cock outlined beneath the silky, black material.

"Hey, dude, come on in. Lookin' good."

Mike followed him, eyeing that perfect ass barely hidden by the shorts. The house as was deserted as John had said it would be, and only a few lights had been left on. Mike thought it gave the place a romantic feel.

"Take off your jacket, get comfortable. If you like, you can switch to shorts. I brought down an extra pair just in case."

"Thanks, man."

John sat down on the couch and watched as Mike slipped out of everything but his T-shirt and briefs before pulling on the pair of red running shorts. Mike realized that they were at least as tight as the pair that John was wearing when they came to a complete stop at mid-thigh. Grinning sheepishly, he wriggled his torso and swiveled his legs a bit, inching the worn fabric slowly up over his skivvies. When he tugged them up over his butt, he heard a stitch pop and blushed as John cracked a broad grin.

"Where'd you get these shorts, dude—our tenth-grade gym lockers?" Mike joked, blushing and making a meager attempt to suppress a great deal of embarrassment.

"How'd you guess, buddy?" laughed John.

"Don't you think we've gotten a little too fat for them?"

"I think they make you look totally hot, Mike. Incredible."

Mike's cock was already halfway hard and showed plainly through the shorts. He was proud of his dick, though, so he made no effort to hide it as he sat down on the opposite end of the couch from where John had flopped to enjoy the show.

They sat facing each other with their legs slightly spread, smiling as each watched the other's cock stiffen. There was an uncomfortable silence as each waited for the other to speak first.

"You know, Mike, I've always thought you were the hottest guy I knew," said John, finally. "Ever since we both started gymnastics at Edison. I'm just sorry I waited so long to tell you."

Mike suddenly felt warmer toward his best friend than he had ever felt before. "Me too, man. I've wanted to tell you how hard I get just thinking about you for over two years now. You've got one of the hottest fucking bodies I've ever seen on anybody."

"I guess we wasted a lot of precious time, dude. But it's all yours now, you know," said John as he leaned back and put his hands back behind his head.

The invitation wasn't lost on Mike. "John?"

"Yeah, buddy?"

"Would you kiss me?"

John broke into a smile as he moved over to Mike's end of the couch and into Mike's arms. Mike pulled the handsome stud toward him and they came together in a brief but heated, passionate clinch. First they kissed just once on the lips. Then their lips met a bit harder, a little deeper. Mike pulled John closer and ran his hands up the back of his tank top as his tongue worked its way even farther into John's hot mouth.

John sank deeper into Mike's embrace as he opened his mouth wider to let in his buddy's tongue. He responded with his own as his hands cradled the back of Mike's head and his fingers ran through his short, blond hair. Their kisses grew longer, hotter, each one lasting for endless moments. They each became oblivious to everything except their urgent desires.

Mike finally broke free. "I've wanted to feel your hot body against mine for so fucking long…"

"Me too, dude. Why don't you slip your shirt off so you can feel it better."

John's gaze was fixed upon the blond stud as Mike pulled off his tight T-shirt, exposing his broad chest and muscular torso, all the way down to where the beef below his waist was pinched by those silky, supersnug shorts.

John then proceeded to remove his own tank top, and the two young men began to kiss again as their powerful chests rubbed together, flesh against flesh, and their rock-hard dicks pressed against each other through the shining fabric of their shorts. Mike ran his hands up and down his buddy's sculpted back and then slipped them down to squeeze the awesome globes of John Wallach's ass. Mike had always thought that John's ass was the sexiest part of him. He could hardly believe that he was lying there with his hands and mouth feeling up every inch of John's incredible body.

Well, thought Mike wildly, not every inch! From the feel of it against his own cock, Mike could tell there were about eight inches still left to explore. He slid his hands reluctantly from John's ass and attempted to work them between their bodies in order to get a grip on his buddy's hard cock. Though there was barely any give to the elastic of John's running shorts, Mike's right hand pushed past his belly and got a grip on that cock as it rose amidst the sweaty, matted pubic hair in the tight confines.

"Here, dude, let me help," whispered John. "I want to get a look at what you got there, too."

He rose to his knees as he slid Mike's tightly packed shorts off over his engorged penis and muscular thighs and then tossed them aside. As Mike lay there naked, he watched John struggle out of his own shorts. He was incredibly handsome. A faint layer of sweat covered his body. His dark hair hung halfway down his forehead in a disheveled state, and the dim light of the room left his deep-set eyes hidden in shadow. As his hard cock flopped free, it fell down against his low-hanging balls, which bristled with dark hairs. The curve was more pronounced than ever, and the head of it was already wet with pre-cum.

He lay back down on top of Mike, making total body-to-body contact. The two naked gymnasts ground their sweaty, muscular bodies against one another as their tongues explored each other's mouths, and before too long, they were bucking against each other like two wild, rutting animals as their passion reached a crescendo. They were lost, completely gone from any kind of rational thought as their hips pounded together and their minds focused only on the flesh and muscle they each embraced. Sweat was flowing freely now and all Mike could think about was this gorgeous body pressed so tightly against his own. The fact that this was also his best friend made everything about what was happening the most intense and wonderful experience of his life. As he pushed his tongue once more into John's frantically sucking mouth, Mike reached down, grabbing John's hard, muscled ass, and ground against him one last time before shooting his first hot load between their tight stomachs to mix with their sweat.

When John felt the searing ball-juice on his skin, he was pushed over the edge and unloaded his own gut-wrenching jism to mix with Mike's.

Neither of the boys moved for a few silent moments as each caught his breath. To their surprise, even after their explosive orgasms, their dicks remained hard and pressed against each other.

"That was the greatest, John," choked Mike. "It was hotter than I ever imagined it would be."

"We haven't even started, dude, and, from the stiffness of your cock, I'd say it agrees."

With that, John got up and moved his head to the slimy mixture of their cum as it began to slide down over Mike's sexy abs.

"You can't imagine how long I've wanted to taste

your cum," John said as he began to lap up the cream that lay there.

Mike couldn't believe how incredibly turned on he got as he watched his best friend swallowing their mixed loads. His cock stiffened right back to its full hardness.

"Yeah, swallow that cum, dude, you're makin' me so fucking hard. Suck on my dick. I've wanted to see your mouth sliding up and down on my cock for so fucking long."

After getting the last of the cum off Mike's belly, John switched his attention to Mike's rock-hard meat. He licked the last few drops of cum off the head and then lowered his mouth over the rigid stalk. His tongue immediately began to slide over the entire surface, tasting every salty square inch of Mike's ever-thickening cock.

Mike leaned back and enjoyed the sight of John's handsome face sliding up and down on his dick. It was amazing how quickly he was rushing back to life. "Whoa, dude! I'm going to shoot if you keep that up, and I'd rather save it for a while."

John smiled slyly as he pulled away from his buddy's cock and leaned back to rest against the arm of the couch.

Mike continued. "You suck dick pretty well. Almost too well. Have you ever done this with anybody else?"

"This weekend was the first time," John lied. Well, maybe it was a half-lie. He *had* usually been a top, but he didn't know how Mike would react if he started telling him about cruising bars on the other side of town for the past couple of years. Giving blowjobs to older men in seedy bathrooms didn't count tonight. Then he proceeded to tell Mike all about that long-lost distant relative of his, Mark Simpson, and everything that had happened on the trip home from the funeral.

"Wow, this guy sounds great. Is he ... you know ... hot?"

"Good-looking? Yeah, he's a real stud."

Mike almost swooned at being able to talk so openly about other guys for the first time in his life. Up until now, he had barely thought about men outside of his own fantasies, let alone discussed what it was he'd been feeling since he could remember. Now there they were, talking about horse-hung studs as if they were at a bar rapping about girls with the other guys on the team. This was great!

"But, hey, I forgot to tell you," John said excitedly, "you're going to get a chance to meet him and his roommates at the state tournament next weekend in Minneapolis. He's invited you and me to spend Saturday night and Sunday with them."

"Far out! I hope his roommates are hot."

"Yeah, dude so do I," John said, "but no matter how hot they are, you'll always be my special fuck-buddy. That is, if you don't mind."

"I don't mind at all, John, that is, so long as you're mine," Mike replied as the two boys stared lovingly into each other's eyes.

"So tell me, dude," John said, breaking the silence, "have you ever made it with anyone before?"

"Yeah," Mike answered shyly, "three people, and they were all just this weekend, too."

"Three people! Holy shit! You're uncontrollable! So tell me, who were they?"

Mike proceeded to tell him about his encounter with Kevin and Scott Gorseth after leaving his place Friday night.

"Oh man! Your own cousin. I've thought he was pretty fucking hot for a younger dude. He's really built himself up since he moved in with your family. Scott Gorseth. Isn't he that really cute looking guy on the wrestling squad?"

"He sure is, and you wouldn't believe the dick he has on him. It's at least nine inches."

"No shit! But that's only two. Who's the third?"

"You won't believe me."

"Try me."

"On Saturday morning I ran into Jason Carmichael. We got stoned on some excellent weed, and—I don't know, man—he asked me to fuck him!"

John couldn't believe what he had heard. "You fucked *Jason Carmichael*?"

"Right there in the back of his van."

"Holy fuck. I can hardly believe it."

"Believe it, dude, he even sucked my dick. Despite his reputation, Jason digs guys obviously as much as he does girls."

"So you fucked Jason Carmichael. Have you ever been fucked?"

"No, man, but I've been curious about it since Saturday."

"You wanna find out what it's like?"

"Yeah, sure," Mike smiled.

"Follow me upstairs." The two naked young men left the living room and headed up the stairs to John's bedroom, their hard cocks slapping against the flesh of their thighs. When they reached his bedroom, John switched on the lamp beside his bed, lighting the room brighter than John wanted, revealing the clothes strewn about, his gymnastics trophies on the shelf, and posters of his favorite sports teams hanging on the wall. A *Playboy* centerfold or two had been taped near his bed—he was a bit more daring than Mike in that department, but then again, he was the more experienced of the pair. He threw an orange towel over the shade, sending the room into an autumnal cast. While he did this, Mike lay back on the full-sized mattress and spread his legs slightly.

John pulled out a small bottle of poppers that Mark had given him and set it on the table alongside his bed.

"What's that?" Mike asked.

"You'll find out." John kneeled onto the bed and crawled up between Mike's legs.

"The first thing we have to do is slick you up." With that, John grabbed Mike by the ankles, pushing them up over Mike's head and exposing his asshole to the air.

"Yeah, John, lick my ass."

John lowered his mouth and began to lick up and down the slightly furry crack of his buddy's butt, running his tongue lightly back and forth over the tight sphincter muscle. The heady smell of Mike's ass proceeded to make John almost uncomfortably hard, so he decided he'd better get right to business, working his tongue into the tight muscle as deeply as he could. It wasn't long before Mike was going absolutely nuts: "Oh, yeah, dude, lick my ass, jam it in. It feels so fucking good. Let me feel your dick in me! Go ahead. Fuck me!"

"You really ready, dude?" John looked up from Mike's ass.

"Yeah, John, fuck me!"

"First, get my dick wet." John scooted up onto Mike's chest until his dick hung over Mike's face. Mike, without hesitating, swallowed his buddy's cock for the first time and began to soak the rock-hard slab of meat with his spit. For so long he had wanted to taste John's cock and now, pretty soon, it would be sliding up his ass.

After a couple of minutes of sheer pleasure, John

pulled his slicked up cock out of Mike's hot mouth and reached over for the bottle of nitrite on the nightstand.

"Here take a quick whiff of this. They're called poppers, and they should keep you from feeling much pain."

Mike took a hit, and then John did likewise before bracing himself with his hands on the back of Mike's thighs and pressing the slick head of his dick up against Mike's tight asshole. Slowly, it gave way as Mike groaned a little, and the head popped in. It was so big—it was almost too much for his virgin behind to take! Mike let out a muffled scream, but now the poppers were hitting him and he couldn't imagine anything more urgent than feeling John's cock all the way up his ass.

"All the way," he moaned, "shove it all the way in!"

John needed no extra coaching. He continued to push in slowly until his pubic hair was brushing up against the crack of Mike's ass, and as the poppers took full effect, he pulled back out and then slammed back in as hard as he could. This was just what Mike wanted, and in his delirious state, he had discovered that John's uniquely curved cock tickled him in a crazy way he had never felt before.

"Yeah, dude, fuck me hard. Shove it in deep." Mike reached down and began to stroke on his own rock-hard erection.

As John's hips pistoned in and out, he lowered his face down to Mike's so that their sweaty chests rubbed together and so their mouths could meet. They kissed each other furiously as their nipples seemed to throw sparks off one another, and the poppers coursed through their brains, forcing them on until John could stand it no longer. He lifted himself from Mike's chest as he jammed his cock, one last time, up to the hilt in his best friend's ass.

"Oh, fuck, Mike, I'm gonna blow!"

"Yeah, dude, shoot it up my ass!"

"Here it comes!" Mike felt the searing heat of his buddy's cum as it shot deep into his bowels. At the first sensation, he started shooting his own load all over his own chest and stomach. Still in his nitrite euphoria and with his fat dick jammed to the hilt in Mike's ass, John leaned over and greedily lapped up the cum that Mike had shot onto his chest.

Then, as the poppers wore off and his cock began to relent, John slipped out of Mike's ass and rolled over beside him. After about ten minutes of silence, their labored breathing abated, and they slipped out of bed to shower together. As the sticky remnants of their orgasms were rinsed away, their lust was enflamed anew, and Mike briefly fucked John in the shower. Afterward, the two boys returned to the bedroom for the continuation of what would turn into a long night of continuous fucking, sucking, and lovemaking.

CHAPTER SEVEN

VII

When they awoke the next morning, after only a couple of hours of sleep, Mike and John found themselves wrapped in each other's arms. Their dicks were pressed warmly against one another, and their sleepy grins betrayed the fact that it was more than the need to take a piss that was making them stiff as iron poles. They kissed and ground those morning hard-ons together as if they'd done it for years, but then John suddenly noticed the clock:

"Shit, Mike, it's already eight! We've got class in half an hour."

"Mmm. Let's skip," purred Michael.

"You know we can't, dude. Gersinski hates jocks, he'd take any excuse to throw strikes against us."

"Shit. Advanced geometry wasn't exactly what I had in mind. We gotta stop taking these sunrise courses," Mike said as he gave John's hard cock a playful squeeze. After a quick shower and a little mutual groping, they reluctantly got dressed.

"You know," Mike giggled, "it's going to be weird seeing Jason today after what happened on Saturday."

"Just play it cool, man. If he thinks you're freaked out he might just pretend that it never happened. Now that would be a real tragedy."

"Why is that?"

"Because it might make it tough to get him into bed with the both of us."

"Are you serious? A three-way with Jason Carmichael!"

"Yeah, sounds hot, doesn't it?"

"Do you think he'll go for it?"

"If you weren't imaging what happened on that old airport road of yours, I can't imagine him *not* going for it."

"Far out!"

"He doesn't know about me yet, so for the meantime let's keep it that way."

"You got it, dude." Mike grinned.

The humpy pair wolfed down a box of Pop Tarts and two quarts of milk, and then it was out the door for a quick jog to school.

The day seemed to stretch out endlessly for Mike as he sat through class after boring class. Most of the time he found himself looking around at the hottest guys in each room, imagining what it would be like to make it with them. During his last class of the day, he found his main target for these boner-producing daydreams to be his fellow gymnast, Dave Sommers.

Dave was really a hot-looking dude. His dark blond hair was fluffy in the afternoon sunlight, and those incredibly sexy hazel-green eyes of his sparkled whenever he looked up to copy something from the board. His face was a chiseled masterpiece with high cheekbones and a strong, jutting jawline. His sweetly sexy, thin-lipped smile, which served double-duty dimpling his cheeks and exposing a perfect set of teeth, only topped off a perfect package.

It was that incredibly innocent and gentle smile that turned this rugged young athlete into the puppy dog that turned Mike Belson on in a way that seemed to be a little different from how other guys got him hard. Though Dave was just about his age, Mike thought of him as younger. Dave hardly ever swore, and he could barely look a pretty girl straight in the eye. When he drank beer, he caught a buzz with just a few gulps, and though he was fantastic on the rings, he never seemed to swagger around like the other guys on the gym squad. Thinking about it this way, Mike decided he would simply just love to break Dave in. God, bagging him would really prove his current, wild winning streak was no fluke. He'd be slow and easy with Dave, kissing him and comforting him through both the pleasure and the pain.

As he stared and fantasized, Mike was suddenly shocked to realize that Dave was staring back—and flashing him that sexy, shy grin of his and not turning away.

Mike panicked and averted his gaze as if Dave could read every seductive thought in his mind. He was friends with Jason Carmichael. Could Jason have told him what happened? Then again, thought Mike, if he did he would have blown his own cover.

Mike didn't look back for the rest of the seminar. When the professor finally relented, Mike walked past Dave's desk and slapped him on the back. "Hey, dude, don't be late for practice. We're gonna have to take it all the way between now and the championship this weekend."

"I'll be there, man," Dave said without quite looking him in the eye.

Gymnastics practice started out with a speech from the coach: "Okay, men, it's only one week now until the state tournament in Minneapolis. We're going to have some tough competition there, so we need to use the next five days to our best advantage. Unfortunately, I have to leave early today. I want you guys to have a full workout, though, so I'm putting Carmichael in charge. He'll run through the final part of your workout. Here are my keys, Jason." The coach tossed them over the heads of the rest of the guys. "You're responsible for getting everybody out of here and locking up the gym."

"You got it, Coach." Jason grabbed the keys and turned toward Mike with a cocky grin on his face.

"Okay, everybody; get to work, now!" the coach shouted.

Jason walked over to Mike as the rest of the guys began warming up. "Hey, dude," he said, dangling the coach's keys, "why don't you hang out with me when we're done? I'll meet you by the showers after practice, when everyone else clears out."

"You've got a deal," said Mike, with little more than an arched eyebrow. He couldn't wait to tell John.

Walking over to the pommel-horse where John was practicing, Mike took spot and watched his buddy's powerful, muscular arms in action until he dismounted.

"What's up?" John asked, a thin trickle of sweat slipping down the side of his gorgeous face.

"Jason wants me to meet him in the shower after everyone else is gone."

"Far out!" John's face lit up, his mind turning cartwheels over the potential of the situation. "You do just what he said and I'll hide out in the equipment room. After everyone else is gone, I'll join you two and we'll give Jason a real run for his money."

Both teammates were visibly turned on by the thought and had to turn away for a few minutes to get the hard-ons clearly showing through their shorts to go down.

At the same time, Jason had wandered over to the weight room where his friend Dave Sommers was working on the bench press: "It's all set, dude. Mike and me will be hanging in the locker room near the showers after I lock up. I think he's really hot for it. The only thing he doesn't know is that he's going to be dealing with two hard cocks besides his own. You sure you're ready for this, buddy?"

"I think so, Jason. Man, I can't wait to see him all hot and sweaty." Dave smiled. "He's got to be the foxiest guy on campus. Do you think he'd mind my horning in on your action?"

"Not to worry my friend." Carmichael gave Dave a sly grin. "I swing both ways, and that's gonna stay that way so long as everyone uses a little discretion. Now, though I really think Mike's sweet on Johnny-man-about-town, the two of them seem to be share-and-share-alike kind of guys, and what's not to like about you? All you have to do is sit in the coach's office like you're waiting for me, and, when everybody is gone, lock the door and join us in the shower."

"You can count on it, dude!" Dave blushed, his eyes glistening with the thought.

After practice, Mike deliberately took his time getting undressed, mainly so he could concentrate on keeping his erection under control. When the last of the team had finished washing off and stuffing themselves back into their requisite tight jeans and muscle-hugging flannel shirts, he finally peeled off his shorts and jock-strap. He hid his fat, semi-erect cock behind a towel before hitting the showers on his own. There had been no sign of John, and Mike figured he was already hiding out in the equipment room.

Alone in the shower, he turned on one of the heads and just stood under the hot spray. The water felt wonderful as it ran down over the smooth contours of his body, and the area filled with steam. He remained that way, loosening the kinks of his work-out under the sweltering deluge, for about fifteen minutes, his only movement being the languid stroking his hands made up and down his solid torso. Then, without warning, the silence was broken.

"Hey, dude."

Mike's cock started to stiffen as he saw Jason stepping through the steam, completely naked and stroking his hard ten inches of meat.

"I'm glad you waited, man," Jason said. "After Saturday, you've given me a real taste for prime beef."

Though the words did him proud, Mike didn't voice anything in return. He just kneeled down in front of Jason and took the senior's hot, hard cock into his mouth. His practice over the weekend had obviously paid off, as he was able to take nearly three-quarters of Jason's awesome rod down his throat. His technique had also improved, as evidenced by the fact that he had Jason moaning in a matter of minutes.

Jason pulled his dick from Mike's devouring mouth after about five minutes. "Lay down, dude, let's sixty-nine."

Jason scooted low first on the hot, wet tiles of the shower room floor and then Mike kneeled over him as he bent down and took that monster cock into his mouth once again. Jason lifted his own head to wrap his mouth around the heavy hung set of cock and balls that dangled over his face.

Mike was so busy plunging his mouth up and down on Jason's bloated cock that he almost didn't see the figure appear in the shower entrance. That shadow out of the corner of his eye was sure to be John, grinning at them, hard and ready to join in the action. What he saw instead, though, just about made him shoot his load down Jason's throat. Standing in the swirling clouds of steam was none other than Dave Sommers, buck naked, eyes shy, and boasting a raging hard-on.

Jason lowered his head from Mike's crotch to see what had interrupted his sweet blowjob. "Hey, dude, glad you could make it. Sorry, Mike, I forgot to tell you I invited a third party to our little meeting. Hope you don't mind."

"Mind? Are you kidding?" Mike nearly fainted with glee. This was simply too much! It was as if some mysterious cock-demon had taken possession of every hot, hard body in town. Keep your body in tune, thought Mike, sharpen up that desire, ask real pretty, and ye shall receive! Folding his big arms behind his back, he swiveled his hips away from Jason's face, and pointed his throbbing, wet, red cock in foxy Dave Sommers' direction. "Come here, Dave. I know you want it. Suck on my dick! I've wanted to see your lips sliding up and down on my cock for so fucking long." He stood up and faced Dave.

Dave's own cock twitched rigidly in the heavy air as he wrapped his tongue around the fat, spongy head of Mike's erection. The musky smell of his crotch combined with the masculine smell of the shower room created an intoxicating effect. Dave had to have more. He started to lick at and under Mike's hefty balls in an attempt to overpower his senses with the smell. Mike moaned as Dave licked at his balls. Reaching over to the shower nozzle that was positioned there, he grabbed onto it with his thick hands. The stream of hot water came down on top of him, soaking the hair on his head and under his muscular arms and down over his well-defined pectorals.

Meanwhile, Jason turned his attention to Mike's sexy, upturned ass. Getting down on his knees, he dive his face into Mike's butt and proceeded to give him one hell of an ass-licking. Mike let out a luxurious moan—and Dave would have too, but that was impossible, since his mouth was stuffed with Mike's eight hard inches of prime dick-meat. Jason licked up and down Mike's ass crack, driving him to new heights of passion, and then he stabbed his tongue deep into Mike's asshole. The feeling was so overwhelming that Mike finally had to thrust his hips forward, almost choking Dave, forcing him to pull Mike's dripping cock out of his mouth and moan with the sheer insanity of what he was doing.

"I can't believe I'm finally doing this," whispered Dave.

"You better believe it, dude," grunted Mike, cocky with lust. "Just keep on doing what you're doing."

"You got it, Mike," smiled Dave.

"Oh, yeah, Jason, fuck my ass!" said Mike. "Go ahead and shove that fuck-rod up there!"

"You got it, buddy!"—and Jason lined up his hard cockhead against Mike's tight hole. He pressed against it slowly and Mike let out a low groan as the head popped through the sphincter and entered the chute. As Jason's dick continued its steady run up his ass, Mike's groans grew louder and more prolonged. He had never even imagined getting fucked before this weekend, let alone by a monster cock the size of Jason's. Now he was wondering whether he could really take it. With each passing moment, every time he was sure it had to be all the way in, he would feel another inch sliding into virgin, still-unravaged portions of his bowels.

"Wow! You can do it, dude," Dave's voice soothed as he rubbed Mike's bloated cock up and down with his palm. "Just take it slow."

After a final minute of agonizing pain, Mike suddenly realized that it did feel better, and he began to welcome the continuing intrusion. When Jason's ten inches were all the way in, Dave went back to sucking on Mike's cock. When Jason's pubic hair was pressed up against Mike's ass, he held it there for a few seconds before he started sliding it back and forth in Mike's tight asshole.

John couldn't believe his eyes as he stepped into the shower and saw his best buddy taking Jason Carmichael's huge dick up his ass while, at the same time, getting a masterful blowjob from the incredibly sexy Dave Sommers. He stood there stunned, not saying a word, as his cock became rigid as stone.

Jason noticed him first. "What the fuck!?"

Mike looked over at his wildly turned-on best friend, and when Dave finally noticed John, he nearly passed out on the flooding tiles.

"Oh, yeah," said Mike, "I forgot to tell you that I invited someone else to our get-together, too."

"Oh man, Wallach!" Dave's voice nearly cracked. "I never would have guessed you dug this kind of action. Say Mike, I know you're kinda busy right now, but he's so damn hot ... would you mind...?"

Mike grinned, wincing a bit at the feel of Carmichael's massive torpedo still wedged up his butt. "Share and share alike, buddy. What are friends for?"

Jason took Mike's cock from Dave's lips, and Dave immediately went for a warm embrace with John. He pressed his wet body against John's and kissed him full on the lips. John kissed back and began to grind his hard cock against Dave's. Jason just laughed and continued to frig Mike's dick and slam his own rod in and out of that firm, willing ass.

After a few minutes of kissing and probing John's mouth with his tongue, Dave began to kiss his way down John's hard, hunky body. When he reached John's pulsing erection, he grasped it gently in his palm, feeling the heavy hang of his fur-covered balls. His eyes glazed over as he stared at the stiff, slightly curved stalk, and his fingers lightly traced the most visible vein up its entire length. The attention John was receiving from sexy Dave Sommers was driving him crazy, and pearly pre-cum started to drip from his enlarged piss-slit. Dave saw the flowing juices and immediately slipped out his tongue to lap them up. From there, he proceeded to take the entire head in his mouth, savoring the salty taste and smooth texture of John's cockhead for almost a full minute before moving down the rigid penis. John, never having dreamed he could have this kind of fun with his own teammates, couldn't get over those sexy lips wrapped around his dick.

"You've got a great rod, man," Dave said with a boyish smile as he let John's cock slip from his mouth. "How'd you like to fuck me with it?"

John couldn't think of anything he'd like to do more. "No problem, man!" he said as he helped Dave up off the floor.

Dave moved over to where Mike was now on all fours, being fucked to the hilt by Jason, and shoved his dick into Mike's face. Mike latched onto it eagerly, taking it as deep into his throat as Jason's dick was deep in his ass.

John moved up behind Dave and slowly worked his eight-inch dick into Dave's tight butt. Dave gasped, his eyes rolling in their sockets, but in a minute or two, he took it like he was used to it and urged John on:

"Go ahead, dude, yeah, fuck me for all you're worth." It was all the encouragement John needed as he slid his hard-on all the way up Dave's fantastic ass.

With the water soaking down the four squad members, and clouds of steam billowing out to obscure the action, a passerby simply wouldn't have noticed anything out of the ordinary. On closer inspection, though, he would have found four gym buddies locked in an orgy of hot, uncontrollable lust. He'd see a handsome blond stud being impaled on the huge dick of a young man with the face of a choir boy. At the same time, the blond stud had his mouth wrapped around the eight, hard inches of meat of another hot, young, well-built teenager who, in turn, was being fucked within an inch of his life by yet a fourth handsome, dark-haired athlete.

Mike couldn't believe it. Here he had Jason Carmichael's incredible cock up his ass and Dave Sommers' gorgeous cock stuffed down his throat. It was an incredible feeling having both holes filled, and he was reveling in it.

At the same time, John was just going nuts as the walls of Dave's hole milked and massaged his sensitive dick. A few minutes was all he could take, and he started to come.

"Oh, fuck, I'm going to shoot," he moaned as he

jammed his dick all the way up Dave's ass and unloaded his hot, milky load. It was all Dave needed to trigger his own orgasm.

"Oh, God, yeah!" he groaned as his face twisted with pleasure and he shot his wad of hot sperm into Mike's greedily sucking mouth.

At the same time that Dave's ropey gobs were washing across Mike's tongue and sliding down his throat, he felt another searing load boiling up his ass as Jason howled, slapped his ass, and let loose with his own sizzling load.

When the three boys had finished coming, they backed off as Mike lowered himself to the hot, wet floor. From his position on the floor, he frantically began working his hands up and down on his turgid pole. He was so fucking worked up that he had to shoot his load at once. The three other teenagers just stood around him and watched in a daze as every muscle in Mike's body tensed and his teeth clenched, and, finally, his cock erupted with a white-hot explosion of cum.

The three boys watched with horny looks in their eyes as Mike's cock splattered his face, chest, and stomach with his hot sperm. The trio of athletes fell on him with abandon and eagerly began to lick the cum off his body. Mike twitched with pleasure as the hot studs gave him an incredible tongue bath. John licked it off his face and was kissing him passionately. Jason busied himself licking up the large quantity that had puddled between his pectorals, while also taking time to nip and bite at his nipples. Dave took care of the rest by concentrating on his belly and on licking clean Mike's still-hard cock.

After cleaning off the last traces of sperm with their tongues, Jason, Dave, and John leaned back against the shower walls while Mike pulled himself up into a sitting position.

"God, that was great, guys," he said. "I never thought gym practice could be so much fun."

"Yeah," Jason laughed, "can you imagine what the coach would say if he found his four star gymnasts fucking one another's brains out in the shower?"

"Have you seen the way he looks at us sometimes?" Dave snorted. "He'd probably ask if he could join us. Seriously, though, guys, this was great. I'm just wondering when we can get together again. I'd like to make up for lost time!" He flashed Mike and John that sexy smile of his.

"How would you like to spend a weekend making it with three guys from up at Minnesota U.?" John asked.

"Sounds fucking wild to me," Jason said.

"I'd sure go for it," Dave agreed. "Where, when, and who?"

"It's this guy, Mark," John said. "He's some distant cousin of mine I met during my Aunt Hildegard's funeral this past weekend. He's hotter than hell and he's got two roommates who really dig guys, too. They live off-campus in Minneapolis, and they invited Mike and me to spend the rest of the weekend after Saturday's tournament. I doubt if they'd mind a couple of extra cocks on the field."

All four teammates immediately began to get hard again and they started to stroke their stirring dicks.

"Man, I wouldn't miss it for anything," Dave said.

"Me neither," Jason agreed, "but right now I have more urgent things to think about." He looked down at his hardening ten inches. "What say we see who can pop their load first?"

"You're on, dude," the other three agreed.

After only a couple of minutes of willful manipulation, Jason came first, followed in quick succession by Mike and John. Then, after a few more minutes before an enraptured audience, Dave shot a hot wad of jism all the way up his hard, rippling torso.

CHAPTER EIGHT

VIII

After their exciting encounter in the shower, Mike and John left school together and headed over to Mike's house. John's mother and father were still out of town at the funeral, and it was decided he would have dinner at Mike's. They found Marge laying out their meals on the table.

"Oh, there you are." She smiled as John pulled off his jacket at the door. "There's cold milk in the fridge. I've got to run. It's time for me to get to my bridge game. Your father already left for the Elks, and Kevin's eaten and gone up to his room, so I'm afraid you two will just have to keep each other company. It serves you right for being so late," she scolded.

"Sorry, Mom, we'll be fine." Mike kissed her on the cheek as she slipped her coat on.

"And be sure to rinse the dishes," she added just before slipping out the door.

"You know," John said, as the door slammed shut,

"I don't think I've ever seen one of your parents for more than thirty seconds."

"So who's complaining? Let's eat."

The two youths devoured the fried chicken, potatoes, and peas Mike's mother had left for them as if they hadn't eaten for a week, washing it all down with a half-gallon of milk. With dinner and dishes done, John leaned up against the kitchen counter and flashed Mike a sly grin.

"Hey, do you suppose we should see what Kevin is up to?"

Mike looked at him skeptically. "Are you hot to get it on with my little roomie?"

John shrugged. "Hell, he's a cute little fucker, and I've always thought he was pretty cool for a young guy ... and, well, shit! He is related to you somehow, so he must be hot, right?"

Mike just laughed. God, was he feeling good lately! "All right, dude, let's go up and see what the little stud is up to."

The two of them sneaked up the stairs and paused outside of Kevin's room. Mike turned the doorknob slowly and silently and pushed the door open about four or five inches. What they saw through the crack gave both boys instant hard-ons. Buck-naked, and spread out on his bed, Kevin was stroking his raging erection as he flipped through the pages of what looked to be a porno magazine. He was oblivious to everything but the rapid up-and-down movement on his throbbing, rock-hard dick.

"Wow, what a great cock!" John said without thinking. Kevin immediately looked over to the door, but never skipped a stroke as he continued frigging his meat.

"Hey, dudes, come on in and let's choke a few bishops."

"This guy scares me!" said John.

"Sorry, Kev, we didn't mean to spy on you," Mike said.

"Yeah, dude, but you sure do put on a wicked show," John added as he walked in and picked up the magazine Kevin had been looking at. "Hey, where'd you get this?" He flipped through the glossy photos of naked young guys engaged in every conceivable form of sexual activity.

"Oh, that's a jack-off mag I borrowed from Scott Gorseth. He has a whole shitload of 'em. In fact I was just thinking that it would be a hell of a lot more fun to act out these pictures than just looking at them. Why don't you guys get out of your clothes?"

Mike and John hardly wasted a second as they stripped off their shirts, unbuttoned their jeans, and slipped their underwear off, exposing their erections: Mike's jutting out from its bush of dark-blond pubic hair, and John's towering over his tangled nest of dark curls.

"Far out." Kevin grinned as the two older guys sat down on his bed. "One of my best fantasies is picturing you guys doing it together. It really is a turn-on knowing that you actually have."

"I've always thought you were pretty hot, too," John said as he reached over and began to stroke Kevin's cock.

"Hey, I have an idea!" Mike lit up. "Since we've all had fantasies about each other, why don't we each take turns telling the other two exactly what we'd like to see them do with each other. And," he added, "we have to do exactly what we're told."

"Wow, that sounds hot." Kevin's cock twitched at the thought.

"You're on, dude," John agreed. "You go first."

"Okay." Mike thought for a second. "First of all,

113

Kevin, I want to see you go down on Johnny-boy here and give him the best blowjob of his life."

"No problem!" Kevin laughed and immediately crouched down and began to lick up and down on John's hard cock with long, wet tongue strokes. When he had it good and wet, the well-hung teenager wrapped his mouth around the flaring head and lowered himself onto the rigid shaft until his lips found John's thick thatch of dark pubic hair. Increasing the pressure slightly, Kevin let the spit-soaked cock slip out of his mouth momentarily. He stared at the glistening shaft for just a second before plunging his mouth back over the cock, where he began to slide his lips up and down rapidly on the slick eight inches of meat.

John moaned as he received the excellent blowjob while Mike leaned back against the headboard, stroking his own cock, as he watched the exciting vision of his muscular little cousin sucking off his best friend. It was an incredible sight!

"Okay, Kevin, suck his balls for a while," ordered Mike.

John let out a short gasp as Kevin abandoned his cock, but he was quickly mollified when the horny wrestler started to suck on and bite at his hairy balls. Kevin swallowed each of the egg-shaped globes one at a time, tickling them with his tongue and scraping them over with his teeth. After a couple of minutes of this, John had slipped into one of his patented lust frenzies, and his cock began to drip with pre-cum.

"Okay, Kevin," Mike commanded, "back to his dick, and make sure you lick up every drop of his cum."

Kevin attacked John's cock again with a vengeance and eagerly licked up every drop of pre-cum that oozed out before once again wrapping his tongue around the thick, curved stalk.

As Mike spit on his own cock in order to slick it up for his hand, he realized that John was just about too far gone to control himself any longer, so he decided on his finale.

"Okay, Kev, now I want you to make him come. And when he shoots, I want you to catch it all in your mouth. But whatever you do, don't swallow it. When John stops shooting, I want you to move up and kiss him and give him his cum back to taste."

If Kevin's mouth had been free, Mike was sure he would have heard him say, "Excellent!" John must also have liked the idea; only a few seconds after Mike said it, he reached down and grabbed onto Kevin's blond head.

"Oh, fuck, I'm gonna come," he shouted as his searing juice began to erupt into Kevin's mouth. Kevin tried valiantly to hold the hot, syrupy liquid in his mouth until John was done. Cheeks pushed out like a chipmunk's, he succeeded in losing only a few drops down the back of his throat and out of the corner of his mouth.

When John was done, Kevin released the cock, still holding the milky fluid that rolled back and forth across his tongue, and lay down on top of John's smooth, muscular torso. With their dicks pressed against each other, the two young men embraced and locked their lips together. As they passionately kissed, Kevin released his salty gift and let it run freely between their mouths.

John's tongue fought with Kevin's as he let the flavor of his own cum sink into his taste buds. After every last drop of sperm had been accounted for by one or the other of the two, they finally broke apart.

"God, that was an incredible sight," Mike said, still stroking his own erection. "I don't think I've ever seen anything hotter."

"Shit, if you think it looked hot you should try feeling it sometime. Your little cuz is one hell of an expert cocksucker."

"Hey, dudes." Kevin laughed, as he sat back against the headboard next to Mike. "I'm always willing to share my talents whenever the opportunity arises, if you know what I mean."

The boys both laughed at Kevin's not-particularly-good pun and then decided that it was John's turn to pick an activity for Mike and Kevin to perform. John's cock had deflated since Kevin's excellent blowjob, but as he thought about what he'd have the two studs do together, it began to get hard again.

"Okay, Kevin," John said, as he came to a decision, "how would you like to fuck your bunkie in the ass?"

"Far out!" Kevin exclaimed, obviously excited by the idea.

"Actually, you have no choice," John went on, "because I'm ordering you to do it. First off, Mike, I want you to get down on your knees and let Kevin eat out your ass."

Mike went along willingly, and soon Kevin was licking up and down the crack of his ass and tickling away at his asshole with his tongue, just as he had done only three nights before in Scott Gorseth's backyard. What would come next, though, would be a completely new experience.

"Okay, that's enough, Kevin," John commanded, obviously getting into his role. "Now I want you to slide your hard dick all the way up your Mike's ass."

Kevin raised his face up from Mike's butt and scooted up behind him. With Mike still in a kneeling position, Kevin pressed the fat head of his cock up against his cousin's slick hole and slowly pushed it in past the tight muscle.

Tensing slightly, Mike willed himself to relax, allowing his little cousin to enter him. Little, hell, he thought to himself, there was nothing little at all about the piece of meat sliding up his ass.

John jumped off the bed and came around to watch from the side. He stroked his own rigid cock as he watched Kevin's dick shove up to the hilt in Mike's butt.

"Okay, Kev, just hold it there for a second—and then start fucking him for all he's worth."

Kevin did just that, pulling back almost all the way and then ramming his cock back in to its root. His powerful wrestler's thighs gave him extra push, and they bulged impressively with each thrust. John noticed that Kevin's tight, muscular ass would "dimple" each time he buried himself to the hilt in Mike's tight asshole. He was really getting off on watching his best friend getting fucked by this tight young athlete. They were both such good-looking, well-built dudes. As they both began sweating from their exertions, John thrilled to their bulging muscles and glowing, shining flesh. The intoxicating sight made him want to stroke his own cock even more fervently.

With each thrust up his cousin's ass, Kevin's balls would slap against Mike's sweaty undersides. "This is so great, Mike. Your ass is so fucking tight!"

"Go to it, little cuz. Jam your fat cock up my ass. Oh, I can't wait to feel your hot cum."

"Yeah, Kev," John concurred, "shoot that load up your big cousin's butt."

With one last thrust the hunky young wrestler buried his dick in Mike's hot ass and, as he threw his head back and the sweaty muscles of his stomach and chest tensed and stood out, Kevin shot the first wad of his shuddering climax deep into Mike's bowels. Several smaller bursts followed—each of which was accompanied by a pleasing set of moans and groans—and then his slimy, snaky, spent cock slowly slipped out of Mike's hole; and Kevin was still.

"All right!" John exclaimed, having enjoyed his private show. "That was fucking hot! I think I know why innocent little Kev was just about exiled from his hometown—you were probably fucking every girl's hot boyfriend, weren't you!"

"Yup," Kevin agreed, "And not giving a flying fuck who knew or who cared. But don't worry, guys, your secret's safe with me."

"Yeah, well, your ass won't be once I turn this around and start ravaging it," Mike cut in.

"I'm counting on it," grinned Kevin. "But, for now, it's my turn to pick something for you two to do."

"Go to it!" John urged.

"Well, do you remember how I said I pictured you two doing it together?"

"Yeah," Mike said. "Do you want to watch us make out?"

"Not exactly. I never finished telling you how, after imagining it awhile, I would start to picture myself in between you two."

The two older boys looked at each other.

"So," Kevin went on, "I've decided to add myself into your performance. I want you to fuck me in the ass," he said pointing at John, "while I suck on Mike's cock."

"It looks like a few rules are being broken," John said, looking at Mike, "but I suppose we could make an exception."

"Shit, it's fine with me," Mike agreed. "I just want a chance to shoot my load. My balls are starting to ache!"

"Well, here's your chance, cuz." Kevin leaned over

and began to chow down on Mike's throbbing eight inches, while simultaneously raising his ass in the air as an open invitation to John.

As John leaned over and started to lick at Kevin's hot, sweaty ass, Mike looked down at his cousin's mouth working up and down on his cock. He had watched Kevin blow both Scott and John and had wondered how it would feel to have his fine-looking young housemate sucking on his own dick. The answer was—terrific! Kevin obviously relished cocksucking and was giving it his all. The sensation of John's lusty licking at his ass only seemed to spur him on.

"Yeah, Kev, suck on your cousin's big cock." Mike moaned. Kevin's wild tongue was driving him crazy. "I bet what you'd really like right now, though, is John's big dick sliding up your ass." Kevin nodded as best he could with his Mike's cock stuffed in his mouth. "Go ahead, John, fuck the shit out of our little wrestler's ass."

"You got it, dude," John said, after licking his lips. "Here it comes, Kev!" And with only that warning, the dark-haired gymnast began sliding his fat dick up the horny eighteen-year-old's ass.

Vigorously fucked at both ends by the two older studs, Kevin could only reach down and start stroking on his own cock. Mike, who had never had a chance to rest up from his fucking by Kevin, was now soaked in sweat, causing his muscles to gleam in the soft bedroom light. At the same time, beads of sweat trickled down over John's large pectorals, as he increased the speed and tempo of his pumping into Kevin's ass. The whole room had been transformed into a moaning, grunting, groaning den of wild, uninhibited sex, and the three young athletes lost all sense of their surroundings as they strove only to satisfy their fiery cravings.

Mike held firmly to his cousin's head, pushing his fingers through Kevin's close-cropped hair as he pounded his hard eight inches into the willing mouth. He continued to moan as he watched his slicked-up rod piston back and forth through Kevin's tightly gripping lips, and his balls slapped happily against his cousin's chin with every thrust.

John was also far gone with lust as he slammed his aching, rock-hard cock back and forth into Kevin's incredibly tight ass. The musky smells of steaming holes, warm cum, and perspiration that filled the room were driving John wild. As he increased the velocity of his fucking, his sweat-soaked torso tightened, becoming more defined as the muscles stood out in relief.

As flushed and excited as the two older boys were, though, it couldn't possibly compare to what Kevin was feeling as he knelt there with one hard cock up his ass and another jammed down his throat. His own hard cock was literally dripping with pleasure, leaking out a little more pre-cum with each one of John's wild thrusts. Kevin, having suspected Mike of harboring a few fun secrets, had dreamed of this moment for months and was loving every minute of it. His only concern was who would come first, Mike or John. He wondered what his cousin's load would taste like.

He got the answer to both questions as Mike shut his eyes and jammed his cock all the way into Kevin's mouth: "Oh, fuck, Kev, I'm gonna come! Swallow my hot load! Oh, yeah, eat my cum!"

As the hot jism rolled across his tongue, Kevin began shooting his own load onto the sheets.

"Sweet Jesus, Kev!" John cried. "I can feel you shooting!" And with that, John buried his cock up to its base and began rapid-firing his wad deep into Kevin's ass.

Catching their breath, John, Kevin, and Mike took a fleshy, slippery shower together, and, grinning ear to ear, made their future plans. As they slipped back into their clothes, Mike told his cousin about next weekend's trip to Minneapolis, and they decided to make arrangements for Kevin and Scott Gorseth to come along. It was turning into one of the horniest, hottest weekends the boys on the gym squad could ever have imagined.

CHAPTER NINE

IX

The rest of the week went by quickly, with the boys all taking advantage of any spare moments they could find to be together. On Tuesday morning before going to class, Kevin sneaked into Mike's room, and Mike finally got the opportunity to plow his little cousin's ass and to swallow his cum.

After their last class, Mike and Dave went over to John's house to work out in his garage which, of course, turned into a hot and heavy fuck-and-suck session. At one point, John was laid out on the decline bench with Dave's hard cock up his ass while Mike jammed his dick down his throat. The boys just managed to get their clothes back on as John's parents pulled into the driveway, having returned from Aunt Hildegard's funeral. Looking at the sweaty, out-of-breath boys, Mr. Wallach decided that maybe the workout equipment would end up getting used after all, and wasn't a waste of money.

On Wednesday, Jason and John slipped off-campus at lunchtime to Jason's van, where they spent the noon break with John's eight-inch meatpole jammed up Jason's hot hole. They had both come twice before it was time to make a hasty retreat for Psych 101.

That night, Mike, John, and Kevin went over to Scott Gorseth's house to start planning the Minneapolis trip. They decided that Kevin and Scott would drive up by themselves in the Belsons' station wagon, meeting the other four boys, who would be coming up with the team on the bus. The horny squad members weren't able to get any further than that, though, before the planning session evolved into a fuck session with each of them stripping and going at each other on the practice wrestling mats in Scott's basement. At one point, Mike found himself pinned flat on the mat with John sitting propped on his face and Scott impaled on his dick. John and Scott were facing each other from their perches on Mike's mouth and cock but were unable to see each other—Kevin was standing between them with his cock in John's mouth and with Scott's tongue probing his ass.

Thursday night, however, was the best. After gym practice, Mike, John, Dave and Jason headed over to Mike's house for a little replay of their Monday afternoon shower session. When they got home, though, they found Kevin and Scott already going at it in the basement. The four older guys sat down and watched the erotic show, cheering the two hunky wrestlers on as they stroked the hard-ons in their jeans.

Kevin and Scott managed to make the scene last almost ten minutes more before their hot and sweaty bodies finally gave out and they shot their loads into each other's mouths. The older men cheered, even as they stripped off their own clothes and joined the sweet pair on the floor for what turned into an all-out orgy. Afterward, Scott said that he thought it was a great way to be introduced to Dave and Jason, whom he knew on sight, but had never met before.

Friday turned out to be a different matter altogether. The teammates were so busy with preparations for the trip that nobody had time for sex. They would be leaving at six o'clock the next morning, and all the gymnasts had to be in bed by ten Friday night. They needed to conserve their strength and to get plenty of rest before tomorrow's big tournament.

Mike was up bright and early at five. After a shower and a quick breakfast, he loaded up his duffel bag with everything he would need for the weekend. Before leaving, he stopped by his cousin's room, where he found Kevin fast asleep. Deciding to have some fun at his little buddy's expense, he slipped his hand under the sheets and began to stroke Kevin's half-hard, naked cock.

"Oh, yeah, Scott," Kevin moaned in his sleep, "you're the best, man ... love you ... just keep it going...."

Mike smiled and chuckled to himself as Kevin reached full hardness. The little bugger was really in love with Gorseth. That was sweet. When Kevin began to buck his crotch in rhythm with his strokes, Mike decided it was time to go.

"Sorry, dude, I'm running late. I gotta take off now," he added a little loudly.

"Not yet, Scott!" Kevin said in a half-sleepy, half-panicky voice as he sat up straight in bed, only now waking up. "What the fuck's going on!" He looked around for Scott but saw only Mike standing over his bed, smiling.

"Wake up call, dude. I have to get going before

the bus leaves. We'll meet you guys in front of the gymnasium after the tournament."

Kevin sat there taking this all in while trying to clear his head.

"Oh, yeah," Mike added with a laugh, "remember to conserve your cum so you're in prime shape when you get there. No beating off!"

Looking down at his rock-hard cock, Kevin had only one reply for Mike: "You fucker."

Around two o'clock that afternoon, preparations were well under way at the house Mark Simpson and his two buddies shared in Minneapolis. Mark had just come back from the beer distributor, where he had purchased four cases of Budweiser. He was busy making room for them in the refrigerator when his roommate, Jeff Burke, came into the kitchen hauling two garbage bags full of trash he had accumulated from the upstairs bedrooms.

The beefy, blond-haired college junior had given up football the previous year, but his body had remained reasonably hard and solid thanks to a Monday-Wednesday-Friday weight training schedule to which he adhered religiously. This morning Mark thought he looked especially good as he cleaned the house dressed only in an old, tight-fitting pair of running shorts that clearly outlined his huge piece of meat and heavy-hung balls. They flopped around freely, unhindered by the presence of any underwear or jockstrap.

"So tell me, Mark," he said as he set down the bags of garbage, "you're not kidding me about this friend of yours and his buddies, are you?"

"I haven't met any of his teammates or anything, but I can tell you that John is one of the sexiest-looking younger dudes that I've ever seen. The fuck session I had with him in that Iowa motel was probably the hottest of my life."

"Far out," Jeff said as he absentmindedly scratched his balls. "Who who are these other guys coming with him?"

"Three of them are other guys on his gymnastics squad, and, get this, he called me last night to ask if it was all right to bring these two sophomore wrestlers with him. He said that they were kind of young, but that they had great bodies and were really into all-guy sex."

"Wow! Fresh meat!" said Jeff.

"So long as they're at least a geeker past legal," chuckled Mark.

"Hmmm, I smell some chicken cooking up this weekend," Jeff laughed as he picked up the trash and hauled it out the back door.

Around six o'clock, Mark's other roommate, Steve McPhail, came through the back door and grabbed a Bud out of the refrigerator on his way through the kitchen. He pushed down the tab and took a deep swig as he sat down on the couch in the living room. His two roommates were watching a football game on television.

"Well, boys," the handsome, dark-haired jock grinned at his buddies, "I just came from the Southern State Regional Gymnastics Tournament down at the gymnasium. I saw your cousin there—he was kicking ass—and his buddies weren't doing too bad either."

"So how are they?" Mark asked.

The dimples in Steve's angular face deepened as he almost broke into a laugh. "I thought they were probably the hottest-looking dudes I've ever laid eyes on. It was all I could do to keep myself from putting the moves on them right there. Are you sure they're all into guys?"

"Must be something in the food." Mark laughed.

"Did you see the two wrestlers?" Jeff asked with obvious interest.

"Wrestlers?" Steve asked.

"Yeah, two of 'em," Mark replied, "John's friend's little cousin and his cousin's best friend."

"My God! This is gonna be an orgy, isn't it?" Steve said as he stretched his thickly muscled arms behind his head. His well-defined chest strained against the skintight tank top he was wearing. "I don't know if I can hold out till they get here." He laughed as he grabbed the quickly expanding crotch of his running shorts.

"Well, you'd better," Mark warned, "because they'll be here in a little while, and I know they'll be expecting action from you boys."

"Don't worry, dude." Steve laughed. "I plan on going through all six of them this weekend."

Actually, the squad members and their younger buddies didn't make it over to their place until about eight o'clock. When they did arrive, though, the three older men were all ready for them. Mark went to the door when he heard the bell ring, and the first person he saw when he opened it was his third cousin, John, who, if anything, looked even better than he had remembered. Standing a little nervously behind him were five guys Mark hadn't met before. "John! It's great to see you, bud! We were getting a little worried that you might not make it."

"We decided to stop and get something to eat on the way over. You know, so we wouldn't have to leave again once we got here," John answered with sort of a shit-eating grin on his face.

"Good thinking." Mark laughed. "Well, why don't you come in, take a load off, and meet my roommates."

Mark ushered the small battalion of young men in ahead of him, noting with pleasure how exceptionally good-looking they all were. He followed them into the living room where Jeff and Steve were still sitting watching television. They had changed into jeans and T-shirts, and both stood up as the young jocks filed into the living room.

Mark pushed his way through the group and proceeded to make introductions, "Guys, first I'd like you to meet my roommates, Jeff Burke"—he pointed to the tall, well-built blond who smiled and nodded his head—"and Steve McPhail."

The handsome, dark-haired gymnast stood and stuck his hand out to John. "You must be John Wallach. I watched your routine on the parallel bars at the tournament this afternoon. It was really fantastic."

"Thanks." John blushed at the attention. These guys were just the way he liked them, big and beefy. "Let me introduce my buddies. These are my friends, Jason Carmichael and Dave Sommers." The two gymnasts shook hands with the three college guys. "This is my best buddy, Mike Belson." Mike turned to John and smiled when he heard him say that. "This is Mike's not-so-little cousin, Kevin, and his friend, Scott."

Jeff was particularly intrigued by the two young wrestlers and came over to shake hands with them immediately. Kevin seemed equally interested in the well-built, stocky blond.

With the introductions out of the way, Steve tried to get things moving right away.

"So who wants a brew?"

A chorus of "I do's" rang out, and Steve asked John and Scott if they'd help him get beers for everyone. The two boys agreed and followed the handsome twenty-three-year-old out into the kitchen. At the same time, Mark asked Mike and Dave to give him a hand taking everybody's overnight bags upstairs to the bedrooms. With everybody else busy, Jeff, Kevin, and Jason took the opportunity to bring enough chairs into the living room for all of them.

Just as they finished rearranging the furniture, Mark, Mike, and Dave returned from upstairs and Steve, Scott, and John came from the kitchen with three beers apiece clutched in their hands. The beers were passed around while everybody took one of the chairs, which had been arranged in a rough circle, and the sound of nine beer can tops being popped was followed by a short, nervous silence until the boys slowly began to make small talk. This went on for a while until Mark finally decided to get things moving in the right direction:

"I don't think you guys came all this way to just sit around, drink some beers and rap. I know what I'd like to do and that's to see some hard cocks!"

A hearty and encouraging roar of approval rose from the crowd.

"But," cautioned Mark, "I want to have time to enjoy the sight of each of you, so I only want to see those cocks one at a time. What I want us to do is to take turns stripping. Each of us will get up and stand in the middle, here, and take our clothes off one piece at a time, while the others watch. And we'll take turns in alphabetical order."

Everybody began to get excited at the thought of a strip show and agreed to the plan. The only one who seemed less than thrilled was Jeff Burke, who had just figured out who was going to be first.

CHAPTER TEN

X

With the encouragement of all the guys in the room, Jeff stood up in the middle of the circle of chairs and slowly began to peel off the skintight T-shirt that had been hugging his broad shoulders, muscular chest, and thick arms. The twenty-four-year-old ex-football jock figured that if he had to go first, he might as well make a show of it.

When his shirt was off, he flexed his powerful biceps for a few moments to the cheers of the crowd, then began to unbutton his super-tight 501's. He'd put on a fair amount of weight since he'd jacked up his right knee last season, but the extra cushion of fat around his waist only added to his sexy swagger. When he spotted Kevin staring hungrily at him, he forced the young wrestler to use his teeth to open the rest of his jean buttons, allowing for the straining mound of his crotch to push its way out. After the last button, he pulled Kevin off him and shoved the

135

jeans slowly down over his bulging thighs before stepping out of them. The boys could all see his fat cock expanding through his underwear, even as Jeff manipulated it with his hands through the thin cotton material.

After playing with himself for a few minutes, he started to peel back his briefs. The first sight was his dark blond pubic hair, followed by the fat head of his dick. He then let his underwear fall to his feet, where he stepped out of them as well.

His audience was entranced as he coaxed himself to full hardness. They were all impressed by the eight-inch length of Jeff's cock, but what really amazed them was how fat it was getting. It was easily the thickest one that any of them had ever seen, and as Jeff sat back down next to Kevin, the teenager couldn't help reaching over to feel it. He got no complaints from Jeff.

Jason was next, and the cocky senior eagerly went at it, proudly baring his smooth, sloping chest. When he got down to his big ten-inch dick, even the guys who knew what to expect gasped as he pulled down his underwear to expose the stiff monster. When he sat back down, Jeff grabbed greedily at the huge slab of meat and Jason reached over to reciprocate.

"Cut it out, guys!" Mark interrupted. "Everybody keeps their hands to themselves until the show's over."

Jeff and Jason reluctantly let go of each other's cocks and sat back in their chairs, nursing their own erections.

Scott Gorseth stood up next, egged on by Kevin and Steve McPhail. The hunky young wrestler slowly stripped off his clothing, seemingly embarrassed by the special attention the older guys were paying to his smooth, muscular young body. He couldn't have been feeling too self-conscious, though, when he pulled back his jockeys and his fat, nine-inch cock popped out, rock hard and ready for action.

As he returned to his seat, Steve, who was next, stood up and, like Jeff, broke the rule and reached out to lightly stroke Scott's cock and balls. The tousle-haired teenage wrestler's wide, green eyes locked onto the dark-haired college stud's smoldering gray eyes and a quiet shudder passed through his body. He sat down a little shaken and very excited.

Steve removed his clothes quickly and silently, staring at everybody with a lusty "I want to fuck you" gaze. He had a light sprinkling of dark hair on his chest and another light trail leading down into his jeans. He wore no underwear, so when he removed his jeans, his nine-inch cock sprang out from his dark tangle of pubic hair, already hard and dripping with pre-cum.

The Belson "family" was next. Kevin first, whooping it up loudly, and displaying his cock proudly to the group of older guys. Mike, going second, was more restrained but, nonetheless, just as obviously excited. As his body undulated, he met each of their eyes and became truly aware of their desire for him. Better than any crowd at any tournament was their unadulterated lust for his body. They wanted him, every part of him, and it was all he could have ever dreamed.

Only Mark, Dave, and John were left in clothing and they were becoming frustrated. Mark moved through his striptease quickly but still gave everyone a good look at his hard eight-inch cock.

When Dave Sommers stood up, though, no one could take their eyes off the gymnast's beautiful face with its sharp cheekbones and dark, heavy eyebrows. They were almost disappointed when it was blocked for a moment by his shirt as he pulled it off. The feeling quickly changed to excitement, though, when they all saw his smooth, powerful chest and slim, rippled stomach. There was almost an audible quiver when he stepped out of his jeans and underwear in one movement and then teasingly stroked his cock to its full nine hard inches.

John was the last, and he knew how eager everybody was to pounce on their neighbor, so, of course, he dragged his strip show on as long as possible. After taking nearly five minutes just to take off his shirt, the guys decided that they had had enough. In one simultaneous lunge, the others attacked him. As Jeff, Kevin, Mike, and Scott each held one of the brawny gymnast's limbs, Dave and Steve proceeded to strip off his jeans and underwear while Jason and Mark cheered them on.

With John naked, Mark gave the go-ahead, and the orgy began.

Steve was the first to move into action. He had just finished pulling off John's underwear when he dived onto the college junior's stiff, eight-inch dick and began to lick it up and down, slicking it up with his hot, wet mouth. John moaned from the sloppy action going on down at his crotch, but only for a moment. His own mouth was quickly stuffed when Dave Sommers thrust his own big dick down his throat.

When the go signal was given, Kevin also didn't waste any time. He'd been fascinated with Jeff's meaty body and meatier cock ever since the ex-jock stud had stripped, and he didn't waste any time wrapping his tongue around the throbbing muscle of love, much to Jeff's delight. Jason came up on the husky blond from behind and, after spreading the hard globes of his ass, started to lick up and down the former football player's crack. Jeff groaned and shot a small spurt of pre-cum onto Kevin's tongue just as soon as Jason worked his tongue into his tight hole.

In the meantime, Mike moved over to where John's cousin Mark was still sitting on the sidelines.

"This is really turning out to be a hot time," he said as he sat down next to the handsome brunette.

"Yeah, it sure is," Mark answered. "When John told me about you guys I didn't really believe you could all be as sweet and good-looking as he described, but you're all better, believe it or not. He especially told me a lot about you. Now I know why he was in such a hurry to get home last week."

Mike blushed slightly. The words were music to his ears. "Well, he told me about his trip home with you, too, and I can tell you you're even hotter in person than I had imagined."

Mark just stared into Mike's smoldering brown eyes before leaning over and kissing him firmly on the lips. Mike received the kiss willingly and, in turn, reached over and began to run his hands and fingers caressingly over Mark's hard, smooth body. Occasionally, he reached down and stroked the stiff, succulent piece of meat jutting up from between Mark's hairy legs.

Down on the floor, Steve McPhail continued to slide his tongue up and over and all around John Wallach's throbbing cock, driving the teenager almost to the brink of orgasm. Just as he was sure he was about to be rewarded with a gob of John's spunk, he felt his own ass cheeks being pulled apart and a strong, hot tongue burrowing into his hole. John's cock slipped from his mouth, and he let out a deep throaty growl. When he turned to see whose tongue had invaded his ass, he saw Scott Gorseth smiling shyly at him from between his buttocks.

Steve turned around, laughing as he pulled the husky nineteen-year-old into his embrace. The two kissed and rolled around on the floor in each other's arms.

"Do you think anyone would notice if we slipped away up to my bedroom for our own private little party?" Steve asked the horny wrestler.

Scott beamed at the suggestion. "I think everybody's too far gone into their own situations to even care." He got up with Steve and they sneaked out of the room of naked bodies, creeping slowly up the stairs to the bedrooms on the second floor.

Outside Steve's room, the two horny athletes stood for a moment, kissing passionately, as their hard cocks ground against each other. Scott was about four inches shorter than Steve, as well as four years younger, and his smooth, light complexion contrasted sensually against Steve's ruddier, slightly hairier, body. Opening the door, Steve led Scott into his room and motioned him onto the bed while he dimmed the light, casting the room into shadow. Having set the mood, Steve turned back to Scott, who was now reclined on the bed. The young wrestler's muscular body was highlighted even more by the shadows playing over the slopes and bulges of his hairless torso while the hard nine inches of his dick stood up straight and proud.

"God, you're a hot little fucker," Steve whispered in a gravelly voice as his own hard cock twitched in anticipation.

Scott's only answer was to reach up and gently take hold of the college boy's hand and pull him onto the bed with him.

By nature, Scott was a bashful boy, but something about Steve really got his juices flowing. He started to deeply and aggressively french kiss the older man.

140

Breaking the passionate lip lock, Steve kissed his way down the hunky teenager's tight torso, licking up the dried, salty layer of sweat and sniffing at the musky patch of hair under his arms. When he reached the penis, it was rigid and already dripping with pre-cum. Holding it gently, he stroked and caressed it while he stared at the large, plum-shaped cockhead with its glistening, flaring piss-slit.

"Suck on it. Please!" Scott begged.

Steve paused a moment longer and then, giving in to his own desires, he leaned down and licked briefly at the tip of the cock. Lifting his head back up, he savored the taste of the healthy wrestler's pre-cum. A thin strand hung between his mouth and the younger man's dick, gleaming in the dim light of the room.

The one taste was all he needed to drive him over the edge. He wrapped his mouth around the head of the boy's throbbing member and began sucking madly at the oozing head for more of the intoxicating juice. Scott let out a sort of purr as Steve gave him one of the best blowjobs of his young life. He was anxious to reciprocate, however, so he motioned for Steve to swing his legs around until his own nine-inch cock was hanging enticingly over Scott's mouth.

Scott first started licking and sucking upon Steve's hairy balls and slicking up the sensitive crack between his legs and scrotum. Only when these areas were soaked with his saliva did he proceed to Steve's hard cock. The fevered exertions of their sixty-nine were making the boys hot and sweaty. The well-defined muscles of Steve's back reflected back and forth in the shadows as it rose and fell in conjunction with the movements of his mouth on Scott's dick.

As each made love to the other's manhood, it quickly became clear they were rushing on to the conclusion of this action. The pressure and pleasure were building to a peak, and the pair pulled themselves even more tightly together until their sweaty torsos ground against each other and their noses were buried in the dank patches of each other's pubic hair.

Scott swallowed the college junior's cock to its base while his tongue attempted to cover the entire thickly veined surface as he felt his own cock being similarly coaxed to the point of explosion. With his own nose buried in Scott's musky pubes, Steve took one deep breath and surrendered as his climax overtook him, releasing one thundering burst of jism after another into the young wrestler's tightly clenched mouth.

Scott received the spunky load with pleasure and, in turn, cried out as he rushed to shoot his own slimy mixture into Steve's greedily sucking mouth.

"That was one of the hottest things I think I've ever seen, guys!"

Steve quickly rolled off Scott as both boys looked into the shadows of the room from where the voice had just come. Stepping out from a dark corner, still stroking his own rock-hard cock, came Dave Sommers with an embarrassed grin on his face:

"Sorry, guys, it's just that I saw you two sneaking up here, and I figured if I followed I could probably see one hell of a show. You guys sure didn't disappoint me."

Steve and Scott obviously weren't disappointed either. Amazingly, and no doubt thanks to their unexpected company, their cocks remained rigid despite having just come.

"No problem, dude!" Steve laughed. "Why don't you join us for round two?"

Dave smiled shyly, but his cock twitched at the

idea, and he jumped onto the bed with the other two studs.

Downstairs, the action had also gotten hot and heavy. Kevin had just finished watching Jason Carmichael getting fucked up the ass by Jeff Burke's massive piece of meat. The senior squad leader had looked as if he was barely able to take it and finally had to ask Jeff to pull out. This didn't deter Kevin, though. It just made him all the more anxious to try taking it up his own ass. He leaned over and licked at Jeff's fat cock, tasting the residue from Jason's ass as he went about slicking it up for the big job ahead. Nonplussed, Jason took up position at Kevin's rear, lubricating it for what he knew would be a tight fit.

When he felt he was ready, Kevin perched above Jeff's massive dick and slowly began to lower himself onto the fat pole. The massive head pressed against the tight muscle, but went no further. Willing himself to relax as much as possible—considering what was pressing at his rear—Kevin made his hole relent enough to let in part of the monster dick-head. With his eyes clenched shut, he forced himself farther down on the thick stalk. Despite the pain ripping through the cocky wrestler's body, he was determined to go through with this. The body-filling thrust was tremendous, but he continued lowering himself onto the college boy's fat dick until it was completely inside him.

"Shit, man," Jeff moaned, "no one's ever been able to take my dick all the way before without screaming."

Actually, Kevin had felt like screaming, but now the pain was fading and was being replaced by an itch that made him want to start sliding up and down on Jeff's huge dick.

"Oh, God, that feels great!" Jeff breathed heavily

as he watched the lean, muscular teenager impaling himself on his cock. "God, you're a hot little fucker!"

"Yeah, well, so I'm told." The huge cock up Kevin's ass was causing the boy to experience a myriad of new sensations. His own dick was as hard as he ever remembered it being. He had to be careful about touching it, though. In his current sensitive state it wouldn't take a whole lot to make him blow his load.

Jason, watching in fascination as the younger guy got fucked, decided it was time to give the eighteen-year-old another challenge. Standing up, he moved over to where the action was and offered up his ten-inch cock to Kevin. Kevin wrapped his tongue around it without hesitation.

"Shit, man, look at what your little cousin is doing!" John exclaimed as he looked up from Mark's sweaty crotch where both he and Mike were busy trying to give the older boy a double blowjob.

Mike couldn't believe what he saw as Mark's fat cockhead slipped out of his mouth. There was his innocent little roomie, not only riding up and down on one of the fattest cocks he'd ever seen, but also deep-throating Jason's monster ten-incher at the same time. What a horny little fucker!

But then he was no slouch himself, he decided, as he rolled onto his back and, raising his legs, allowed Mark to press his dick up against his asshole. With just a slight push, the head popped in and the college jock's hard cock slid all the way up Mike's willing chute.

Mike would have let out a whimper, but before he could, he found John's musky ass being lowered onto his face. Instead he used his tongue to start reaming out his best buddy's hole.

John's whole body shook with excitement as

Mike's tongue played over his sensitive crack, and his fist flew up and down on his own rigid eight inches. To add to the excitement, every time Mark drove his cock up Mike's butt to the hilt, Mike's tongue would drive just a little deeper into John's ass.

For his part, Mark couldn't believe he was involved in the hot three-way with two sexy, straight-acting gym buddies. It only made it hotter to think that one of them was somehow related to him. The whole scene was getting to be too much, and he knew that pretty soon he would have to come. What eventually set him off, though, was the action going on across the room.

Kevin was still impaled on Jeff's fat cudgel and his tight, young ass was driving the big ex-jock into a frenzy. Hardly anyone had ever been able to take his monster dick up their ass before, much less ride up and down on it, and the new sensations had driven him over the edge. With a howl that caught everyone's attention, he grabbed Kevin by the waist, slamming him all the way down on his cock, and unloaded his steaming balls deep into the younger man's bowels.

When he heard Jeff scream, Jason pulled his own slick cock out of Kevin's mouth and, using his hand to finish the job, worked himself to his own climax. With one deep grunt, he shot his load all over Kevin's face and into his wide-open mouth.

At the same time that he felt Jeff shooting up his ass and Jason starting to splatter his face, Kevin let his own load go, spraying it in full force over Jeff's sweaty chest.

Watching all that flying cum was too much for Mark, as he shoved his own cock up to the hilt in Mike's steaming hole and unloaded his own barrage of ball juice.

From his perch on top of Mike's face, John wasn't aware of much else besides the incredible pleasure that was centered on his asshole. He did, however, see the contortions of ecstasy spreading over Mark's face and realized this guy was coming deep inside his best buddy's ass. The thought turned him on so much that, within seconds, he was shooting his own hot load of jism all over Mike's sweaty, muscular torso.

Mike was now the only one of the six guys who hadn't come yet. As the others gathered to stand around him as he lay on the floor, he scooped a handful of John's hot cum off his chest and used it to slick up his straining, rock-hard cock. With a glazed look in his eyes as he stared around at all the hot, sexy young guys standing over him, he began to perform a private jack-off show for them. Raising his hips off the floor, he sluiced his organ through both of his cum-slicked hands. The guys standing there all started to get hard again from the sexy show at their feet. Indeed, despite the fact that they had all just come, they began jacking off as they watched with silent fascination.

Mike's whole body was undulating as he sank deeper and deeper into horny intoxication, becoming more and more oblivious to the group standing around him, and yet relishing their being there, gazing hungrily upon him. His whole body was bathed in sweat and his biceps bulged as both hands played up and down on his straining cock.

Finally, with his crotch in the air and his head tilted back, Mike let loose with a gut-wrenching growl as he came. The first load shot up at least three feet before falling back down across his face. The screaming jet was followed by two more bursts, equally strong, as well as a whole slew of diminishing weaker spurts.

When it was over, he collapsed on the ground, his body coated with cum. The rest of the guys gave him a spontaneous round of applause so thunderous that Mike was forced to focus his eyes, look up, and smile. This was definitely going to be one of the greatest weekends of his life.

The Masquerade
Erotic Newsletter

◆ ◆ ◆ ◆ ◆ ◆ ◆ ◆ ◆ ◆ ◆ ◆ ◆ ◆ ◆ ◆ ◆ ◆

FICTION, ESSAYS, REVIEWS, PHOTOGRAPHY, INTERVIEWS, EXPOSÉS, AND MUCH MORE!

"One of my favorite sex zines featuring some of the best articles on erotica fetishes, sex clubs and the politics of porn." —*Factsheet Five*

"I recommend a subscription to *The Masquerade Erotic Newsletter*.... They feature short articles on "the scene"...an occasional fiction piece, and reviews of other erotic literature. Recent issues have featured intelligent prose by the likes of Trish Thomas, David Aaron Clark, Pat Califia, Laura Antoniou, Lily Burana, John Preston, and others.... it's good stuff." —*Black Sheets*

"A classy, bi-monthly magazine..." —*Betty Paginated*

"It's always a treat to see a copy of *The Masquerade Erotic Newsletter,* for it brings a sophisticated and unexpected point of view to bear on the world of erotica, and does this with intelligence, tolerance, and compassion." —Martin Shepard, co-publisher, The Permanent Press

"Publishes great articles, interviews and pix which in many cases are truly erotic and which deal non-judgementally with the full array of human sexuality, a far cry from much of the material which passes itself off under that title.... *Masquerade Erotic Newsletter* is fucking great." —*Eddie, the Magazine*

"We always enjoy receiving your *Masquerade Newsletter* and seeing the variety of subjects covered...." —*body art*

"*Masquerade Erotic Newsletter* is probably the best newsletter I have ever seen." —*Secret International*

"The latest issue is absolutely lovely. Marvelous images...." —*The Boudoir Noir*

"I must say that the *Newsletter* is fabulous...."
—Tuppy Owens,
Publisher, Author, Sex Therapist

"Fascinating articles on all aspects of sex..." —*Desire*

◆ ◆ ◆ ◆ ◆ ◆ ◆ ◆ ◆ ◆ ◆ ◆ ◆ ◆ ◆ ◆ ◆ ◆

Free GIFT

BADBOY

JOHN PRESTON

Tales from the Dark Lord II $4.95/176-4

The second volume of acclaimed eroticist John Preston's masterful short stories. Also includes an interview with the author, and an explicit screenplay written for pornstar Scott O'Hara. An explosive collection from one of erotic publishing's most fertile imaginations.

Tales from the Dark Lord $5.95/323-6

A new collection of twelve stunning works from the man *Lambda Book Report* called "the Dark Lord of gay erotica." The relentless ritual of lust and surrender is explored in all its manifestations in this heart-stopping triumph of authority and vision from the Dark Lord!

The Arena $4.95/3083-0

There is a place on the edge of fantasy where every desire is indulged with abandon. Men go there to unleash beasts, to let demons roam free, to abolish all limits. At the center of each tale are the men who serve there, who offer themselves for the consummation of any passion, whose own bottomless urges compel their endless subservience.

The Heir•The King $4.95/3048-2

The ground-breaking novel *The Heir*, written in the lyric voice of the ancient myths, tells the story of a world where slaves and masters create a new sexual society. This edition also includes a completely original work, *The King*, the story of a soldier who discovers his monarch's most secret desires. Available only from Badboy.

Mr. Benson $4.95/3041-5

A classic erotic novel from a time when there was no limit to what a man could dream of doing.... Jamie is an aimless young man lucky enough to encounter Mr. Benson. He is soon led down the path of erotic enlightenment, learning to accept cruelty as love, anguish as affection, and this man as his master. From an opulent penthouse to the infamous Mineshaft, Jamie's incredible adventures never fail to excite—especially when the going gets rough! First serialized in *Drummer*, *Mr. Benson* became an immediate classic that inspired many imitators. Preston's knockout novel returns to claim the territory it mapped out years ago. The first runaway success in gay SM literature, *Mr. Benson* is sure to inspire further generations.

THE MISSION OF ALEX KANE

Sweet Dreams $4.95/3062-8

It's the triumphant return of gay action hero Alex Kane! This classic series has been revised and updated especially for Badboy, and includes loads of raw action. In *Sweet Dreams*, Alex travels to Boston where he takes on a street gang that stalks gay teenagers. Mighty Alex Kane wreaks a fierce and terrible vengeance on those who prey on gay people everywhere!

Golden Years $4.95/3069-5

When evil threatens the plans of a group of older gay men, Kane's got the muscle to take it head on. Along the way, he wins the support—and very specialized attentions—of a cowboy plucked right out of the Old West. But Kane and the Cowboy have a surprise waiting for them....

Deadly Lies $4.95/3076-8

Politics is a dirty business and the dirt becomes deadly when a political smear campaign targets gay men. Who better to clean things up than Alex Kane! Alex comes to protect the dreams, and lives, of gay men imperiled by lies.

Stolen Moments $4.95/3098-9

Houston's evolving gay community is victimized by a malicious newspaper editor who is more than willing to sacrifice gays on the altar of circulation. He never counted on Alex Kane, fearless defender of gay dreams and desires everywhere.

Secret Danger $4.95/111-X

Homophobia: a pernicious social ill hardly confined by America's borders. Alex Kane and the faithful Danny are called to a small European country, where a group of gay tourists is being held hostage by ruthless terrorists. Luckily, the Mission of Alex Kane stands as firm foreign policy.

Lethal Silence $4.95/125-X

The Mission of Alex Kane thunders to a conclusion. Chicago becomes the scene of the right-wing's most noxious plan—facilitated by unholy political alliances. Alex and Danny head to the Windy City to take up battle with the mercenaries who would squash gay men underfoot.

JAY SHAFFER

Shooters $5.95/284-1

A new set of stories from the author of the best-selling erotic collections *Wet Dreams, Full Service* and *Animal Handlers*. No mere catalog of random acts, *Shooters* tells the stories of a variety of stunning men and the ways they connect in sexual and non-sexual ways. A virtuoso storyteller, Shaffer always gets his man.

Animal Handlers $4.95/264-7

Another volume from a master of scorching fiction. In Shaffer's world, each and every man finally succumbs to the animal urges deep inside. And if there's any creature that promises a wild time, it's a beast who's been caged for far too long.

Full Service $4.95/150-0

A baker's dirty dozen from the author of *Wet Dreams*. Wild men build up steam until they finally let loose. No-nonsense guys bear down hard on each other as they work their way toward release in this finely detailed assortment of masculine fantasies.

Wet Dreams $4.95/142-X

These tales take a hot look at the obsessions that keep men up all night—from simple skin-on-skin to more unusual pleasures. Provocative and affecting, this is a night of dreams you won't forget in the morning.

D.V. SADERO

Revolt of the Naked $4.95/261-2

In a distant galaxy, there are two classes of humans: Freemen and Nakeds. Freemen are full citizens in this system, which allows for the buying and selling of Nakeds at whim. Nakeds live only to serve their Masters, and obey every sexual order with haste and devotion. Until the day of revolution—when an army of sex toys rises in anger....

In the Alley $4.95/144-6

Twenty cut-to-the-chase yarns inspired by the all-American male. Hardworking men—from cops to carpenters—bring their own special skills and impressive tools to the most satisfying job of all: capturing and breaking the male sexual beast. Hot, incisive and way over the top!

GARY BOWEN

Man Hungry $5.95/374-0

By the author of *Diary of a Vampire*. A riveting collection of stories from one of gay erotica's new stars. Dipping into a variety of genres, Bowen crafts tales of lust unlike anything being published today. Men of every type imaginable—and then some—work up a sweat for readers whose lusts know no bounds.

KYLE STONE

Hot Bauds $5.95/285-X

The author of *Fantasy Board* and *The Initiation of PB 500* combed cyberspace for the hottest fantasies of the world's horniest hackers. From bulletin boards called Studs, The Mine Shaft, Back Door and the like, Stone has assembled the first collection of the raunchy erotica so many gay men cruise the Information Superhighway for. Plug in—and get ready to download....

Fantasy Board $4.95/212-4

The author of the scalding sci-fi adventures of PB 500 explores the more foreseeable future—through the intertwined lives (and private parts) of a collection of randy computer hackers. On the Lambda Gate BBS, every hot and horny male is in search of a little virtual satisfaction.contented.

The Citadel $4.95/198-5

The thundering sequel to *The Initiation of PB 500*. Having proven himself worthy of his stunning master, Micah—now known only as '500'—will face new challenges and hardships after his entry into the forbidding Citadel. Only his master knows what awaits—and whether Micah will again distinguish himself as the perfect instrument of pleasure....

Rituals $4.95/168-3

Via a computer bulletin board, a young man finds himself drawn into a series of sexual rites that transform him into the willing slave of a mysterious stranger. Gradually, all vestiges of his former life are thrown off, and he learns to live for his Master's touch.... A high-tech fable of sexual surrender.

The Initiation PB 500 $4.95/141-1

He is a stranger on their planet, unschooled in their language, and ignorant of their customs. But this man, Micah—now known only by his number—will soon be trained in every last detail of erotic personal service. And, once nurtured and transformed into the perfect physical specimen, he must begin proving himself worthy of the master who has chosen him.... A scalding sci-fi epic, continued in *The Citadel*.

PHIL ANDROS

The Joy Spot $5.95/301-5

"Andros gives to the gay mind what Tom of Finland gives the gay eye—this is archetypal stuff. There's none better."

—John F. Karr, *Manifest Reader*

A classic from one of the founding fathers of gay porn. *The Joy Spot* looks at some of Andros' favorite types—cops, servicemen, truck drivers—and the sleaze they love. Nothing's too rough, and these men are always ready. So get ready to give it up—or have it taken by force!

ROBERT BAHR

Sex Show $4.95/225-6

Luscious dancing boys. Brazen, explicit acts. Unending stimulation. Take a seat, and get very comfortable, because the curtain's going up on a show no discriminating appetite can afford to miss. And the award for Best Performer...is up to you....

"BIG" BILL JACKSON

Eighth Wonder
$4.95/200-0

"Big" Bill Jackson's always the randiest guy in town—no matter what town he's in. From the bright lights and back rooms of New York to the open fields and sweaty bods of a small Southern town, "Big" Bill always manages to cause a scene, and the more actors he can involve, the better! Like the man's name says, he's got more than enough for everyone, and turns nobody down....

JASON FURY

The Rope Above, the Bed Below
$4.95/269-8

The irresistible Jason Fury returns—and if you thought his earlier adventures were hot, this volume will blow you away! Once again, our built, blond hero finds himself in the oddest—and most compromising—positions imaginable.

Eric's Body
$4.95/151-9

Meet Jason Fury—blond, blue-eyed and up for anything. Perennial favorites in the gay press, Fury's sexiest tales are collected in book form for the first time. Ranging from the bittersweet to the surreal, these stories follow the irresistible Jason through sexual adventures unlike any you have ever read....

JOHN ROWBERRY

Lewd Conduct
$4.95/3091-1

Flesh-and-blood men vie for power, pleasure and surrender in each of these feverish stories, and no one walks away from his steamy encounter unsated. Rowberry's men are unafraid to push the limits of civilized behavior in search of the elusive and empowering conquest.

LARS EIGHNER

Whispered in the Dark
$5.95/286-8

Lars Eighner continues to produce gay fiction whose quality rivals the best in the genre. *Whispered in the Dark* continues to demonstrate Eighner's unique combination of strengths: poetic descriptive power, an unfailing ear for dialogue, and a finely tuned feeling for the nuances of male passion. *Whispered in the Dark* reasserts Eighner's claim to mastery of the gay erotica genre.

American Prelude
$4.95/170-5

Another volume of irresistible Eighner tales. Praised by *The New York Times*, Eighner is widely recognized as one of our best, most exciting gay writers. What the *Times* won't admit, however, is that he is also one of gay erotica's true masters—and *American Prelude* shows why.

Bayou Boy
$4.95/3084-9

Another collection of well-tuned stories from one of our finest writers. Witty and incisive, each tale explores the many ways men work up a sweat in the steamy Southwest. *Bayou Boy* also includes the "Houston Streets" stories—sexy, touching tales of growing up gay in a fast-changing world. Street smart and razor sharp—and guaranteed to warm the coldest night!

B.M.O.C.
$4.95/3077-6

In a college town known as "the Athens of the Southwest," studs of every stripe are up all night—studying, naturally. In *B.M.O.C.*, Lars Eighner includes the very best of his short stories, sure to appeal to the collegian in every man. Relive university life the way it was *supposed* to be, with a cast of handsome honor students majoring in Human Homosexuality.

CALDWELL/EIGHNER

QSFx2   **$5.95/278-7**

One volume of the wickedest, wildest, other-worldliest yarns from two master storytellers—Clay Caldwell and Lars Eighner, the highly-acclaimed author of *Travels With Lizbeth*. Both eroticists take a trip to the furthest reaches of the sexual imagination, sending back ten stories proving that as much as things change, one thing will always remain the same....

AARON TRAVIS

In the Blood   **$5.95/283-3**

Written when Travis had just begun to explore the true power of the erotic imagination, these stories laid the groundwork for later masterpieces. Among the many rewarding rarities included in this volume: "In the Blood"—a heart-pounding descent into sexual vampirism, written with the furious erotic power that has distinguished Travis' work from the beginning.

The Flesh Fables   **$4.95/243-4**

One of Travis' best collections, finally rereleased. *The Flesh Fables* includes "Blue Light," his most famous story, as well as other masterpieces that established him as the erotic writer to watch. And watch carefully, because Travis always buries a surprise somewhere beneath his scorching detail....

Slaves of the Empire   **$4.95/3054-7**

The return of an undisputed classic from this master of the erotic genre. "*Slaves of the Empire* is a wonderful mythic tale. Set against the backdrop of the exotic and powerful Roman Empire, this wonderfully written novel explores the timeless questions of light and dark in male sexuality. Travis has shown himself expert in manipulating the most primal themes and images. The locale may be the ancient world, but these are the slaves and masters of our time...."

                                                —John Preston

Big Shots   **$4.95/112-8**

Two fierce tales in one electrifying volume. In *Beirut,* Travis tells the story of ultimate military power and erotic subjugation; *Kip*, Travis' hypersexed and sinister take on *film noir*, appears in unexpurgated form for the first time—including the final, overwhelming chapter. Unforgettable acts and relentless passions dominate these chronicles of unimaginable lust—as seen from the points of view of raging, powerful men, and the bottomless submissives who yield to their desires. From a legendary talent comes one of our rawest, most unrelenting titles.

Exposed   **$4.95/126-8**

A volume of shorter Travis tales, each providing a unique glimpse of the horny gay male in his natural environment! Cops, college jocks, ancient Romans—even Sherlock Holmes and his loyal Watson—cruise these pages, fresh from the throbbing pen of one of our hottest authors.

Beast of Burden   **$4.95/105-5**

Five ferocious tales from a master of lascivious prose. Innocents surrender to the brutal sexual mastery of their superiors, as taboos are shattered and replaced with the unwritten rules of masculine conquest. Intense, extreme—and totally Travis.

CLAY CALDWELL

Ask Ol' Buddy   **$5.95/346-5**

One of the most popular novels of this legendary gay eroticist. Set in the underground SM world, Caldwell takes you on a journey of discovery—where men initiate one another into the secrets of the rawest sexual realm of all. And when each stud's initiation is complete, he takes his places among the masters—eager to take part in the training of another hungry soul...

Service, Stud $5.95/336-8
From the author of the sexy sci-fi epic *All-Stud*, comes another look at the gay future. The setting is the Los Angeles of a distant future. Here the all-male populace is divided between the served and the servants—an arrangement guaranteeing the erotic satisfaction of all involved. Until one young stud challenges authority, and the sexual rules it so rigidly enforces....

Stud Shorts $5.95/320-1
"If anything, Caldwell's charm is more powerful, his nostalgia more poignant, the horniness he captures more sweetly, achingly acute than ever."
—Aaron Travis

A new collection of this legendary writer's latest sex-fiction. With his customary candor, Caldwell tells all about cops, cadets, truckers, farmboys (and many more) in these dirty jewels.

Tailpipe Trucker $5.95/296-5
With *Tailpipe Trucker*, Clay Caldwell set the cornerstone of "trucker porn"—a story revolving around the age-old fantasy of horny men on the road. In prose as free and unvarnished as a cross-country highway, Caldwell tells the truth about Trag and Curly—two men hot for the feeling of sweaty manflesh.

Queers Like Us $4.95/262-0
"This is Caldwell at his most charming."
—Aaron Travis

For years the name Clay Caldwell has been synonymous with the hottest, most finely crafted gay tales available. *Queers Like Us* is one of his best: the story of a randy mailman's trek through a landscape of willing, available studs.

All-Stud $4.95/104-7
An incredible, erotic trip into the gay future. This classic, sex-soaked tale takes place under the watchful eye of Number Ten: an omniscient figure who has decreed unabashed promiscuity as the law of his all-male land. Men exist to serve men, and all surrender to state-sanctioned fleshly indulgence.

HODDY ALLEN
Al $5.95/302-3
Al is a remarkable young man. With his long brown hair, bright green eyes and eagerness to please, many would consider him the perfect submissive. Many would love to mark him as their own—but it is at that point that Al stops. One day Al relates the entire astounding tale of his life....

KEY LINCOLN
Submission Holds $4.95/266-3
A bright young talent unleashes his first collection of gay erotica. From tough to tender, the men between these covers stop at nothing to get what they want. These sweat-soaked tales show just how bad boys can really get....

TOM BACCHUS
Rahm $5.95/315-5
A volume spanning the many ages of hardcore queer lust—from Creation to the modern day. The imagination of Tom Bacchus brings to life an extraordinary assortment of characters, from the Father of Us All to the cowpoke next door, the early gay literati to rude, queercore mosh rats. No one is better than Bacchus at staking out sexual territory with a swagger and a sly grin.

Bone $4.95/177-2

Queer musings from the pen of one of today's hottest young talents. A fresh outlook on fleshly indulgence yields more than a few pleasant surprises. Horny Tom Bacchus maps out the tricking ground of a new generation.

VINCE GILMAN

The Slave Prince $4.95/199-3

A runaway royal learns the true meaning of power when he comes under the hand of Korat—a man well-versed in the many ways of subjugating a young man to his relentless sexual appetite.

BOB VICKERY

Skin Deep $4.95/265-5

Talk about "something for everyone!" *Skin Deep* contains so many varied beauties no one will go away unsatisfied. No tantalizing morsel of manflesh is overlooked—or left unexplored! Beauty may be only skin deep, but a handful of beautiful skin is a tempting proposition.

EDITED BY DAVID LAURENTS

Wanderlust: Homoerotic Tales of Travel $5.95/395-3

A volume dedicated to the special pleasures of faraway places. Gay men have always had a special interest in travel—and not only for the scenic vistas. Including work by such renowned writers as Michael Lassell, Felice Picano, Aaron Travis and Lars Eighner, *Wanderlust* celebrates the freedom of the open road, and the allure of men who stray from the beaten path....

The Badboy Book of Erotic Poetry $5.95/382-1

Over fifty of gay literature's biggest talents are here represented by their hottest verse. Both learned and stimulating, *The Badboy Book of Erotic Poetry* restores eros to its rightful place of honor in contemporary gay writing.

JAMES MEDLEY

Huck and Billy $4.95/245-0

Young love is always the sweetest, always the most sorrowful. Young lust, on the other hand, knows no bounds—and is often the hottest of one's life! Huck and Billy explore the desires that course through their young male bodies, determined to plumb the lusty depths of passion. Sweet and hot. Very hot.

LARRY TOWNSEND

Beware the God Who Smiles $5.95/321-X

A torrid time-travel tale from one of gay erotica's most notorious writers. Two lusty young Americans are transported to ancient Egypt—where they are embroiled in regional warfare and taken as slaves by marauding barbarians. The key to escape from this brutal bondage lies in their own rampant libidos, and urges as old as time itself.

The Construction Worker $5.95/298-1

A young, hung construction worker is sent to a building project in Central America, where he is shocked to find some ancient and unusual traditions in practice. In this isolated location, man-to-man sex is the accepted norm. The young stud quickly fits right in (and quite snugly)—until he senses that beneath the constant sexual shenanigans there moves an almost supernatural force. Soon, nothing is what it seems....

2069 Trilogy (This one-volume collection only $6.95) 244-2

For the first time, Larry Townsend's early science-fiction trilogy appears in one volume! Set in a future world, the *2069 Trilogy* includes the tight plotting and shameless male sexual pleasure that established him as one of gay erotica's first masters. This special one-volume edition available only from Badboy.

Mind Master   **$4.95/209-4**

Who better to explore the territory of erotic dominance and submission than
an author who helped define the genre—and knows that ultimate mastery
always transcends the physical.

The Long Leather Cord   **$4.95/201-9**

Chuck's stepfather is an enigma: never lacking in money or clandestine male
visitors with whom he enacts intense sexual rituals. As Chuck comes to terms
with his own savage desires, he begins to unravel his stepfather's mystery.

Man Sword   **$4.95/188-8**

The *tres gai* tale of France's King Henri III. Unimaginably spoiled by his
mother—the infamous Catherine de Medici—Henri is groomed from a young
age to assume the throne of France. Along the way, he encounters enough
sexual schemers and randy politicos to alter one's picture of history forever!

The Faustus Contract   **$4.95/167-5**

*Two attractive young men desperately need $1000. Will do anything. Travel OK.
Danger OK. Call anytime...* Two cocky young hustlers get more than they bar-
gained for in this story of lust and its discontents.

The Gay Adventures of Captain Goose   **$4.95/169-1**

The hot and tender young Jerome Gander is sentenced to serve aboard the
H.M.S. Faerigold—a ship manned by the most hardened, unrepentant criminals.
In no time, Gander becomes well-versed in the ways of men at sea, and the
Faerigold becomes the most notorious ship of its day.

Chains   **$4.95/158-6**

Picking up street punks has always been risky, but in Larry Townsend's classic
Chains, it sets off a string of events that must be read to be believed. One of
Townsend's most remarkable works.

Kiss of Leather   **$4.95/161-6**

A look at the acts and attitudes of an earlier generation of leathermen, *Kiss of
Leather* is full to bursting with the gritty, raw action that has distinguished
Townsend's work for years. Pain and pleasure mix in this tightly-plotted tale.

Run No More   **$4.95/152-7**

The continuation of Larry Townsend's legendary *Run, Little Leather Boy*.
This volume follows the further adventures of Townsend's leatherclad narra-
tor as he travels every sexual byway available to the S/M male.

Run, Little Leather Boy   **$4.95/143-8**

The classic story of one young man's sexual awakening. A chronic under-
achiever, Wayne seems to be going nowhere fast. When his father puts him to
work for a living, Wayne soon finds himself bored with the everyday—and
increasingly drawn to the masculine intensity of a dark sexual underground....

The Scorpius Equation   **$4.95/119-5**

Set in the far future, *The Scorpius Equation* is the story of a man caught
between the demands of two galactic empires. Our randy hero must match
wits—and more—with the incredible forces that rule his world.

The Sexual Adventures of Sherlock Holmes   **$4.95/3097-0**

Holmes' most satisfying adventures, from the unexpurgated memoirs of the
faithful Mr. Watson. "A Study in Scarlet" is transformed to expose Mrs.
Hudson as a man in drag, the Diogenes Club as an S/M arena, and clues only
Sherlock Holmes could piece together. A baffling tale of sex and mystery.

F L E D E R M A U S

Flederfiction: Stories of Men and Torture   **$5.95/355-4**

Fifteen blistering paeans to men and their suffering. Fledermaus unleashes
his most thrilling tales of punishment in this special volume designed with
Badboy readers in mind. No less an authority than Larry Townsend intro-
duces this volume of Fledermaus' best work.

DONALD VINING

Cabin Fever and Other Stories $5.95/338-4

Eighteen blistering stories in celebration of the most intimate of male bonding. From Native Americans to Buckingham Palace sentries, suburban husbands to kickass bikers—time after time, Donald Vining's men succumb to nature, and reaffirm both love and lust in modern gay life.

Praise for Donald Vining:

"Realistic but upbeat, blunt but graceful, serious but witty... demonstrates the wisdom experience combined with insight and optimism can create."
—*Bay Area Reporter*

DEREK ADAMS

My Double Life $5.95/314-7

Every man leads a double life, dividing his hours between the mundanities of the day and the outrageous pursuits of the night. In this, his second collection of stories, the author of *Boy Toy* and creator of sexy P.I. Miles Diamond shines a little light on what men do when no one's looking.

Boy Toy $4.95/260-4

Poor Brendan Callan—sent to the Brentwood Academy against his will, he soon finds himself the guinea pig of a crazed geneticist. Brendan becomes irresistibly alluring—a talent designed for endless pleasure, but coveted by others for the most unsavory means....

Heat Wave $4.95/159-4

"His body was draped in baggy clothes, but there was hardly any doubt that they covered anything less than perfection.... His slacks were cinched tight around a narrow waist, and the rise of flesh pushing against the thin fabric promised a firm, melon-shaped ass...."

Miles Diamond and the Demon of Death $4.95/251-5

Derek Adams' gay gumshoe returns for further adventures. Miles always finds himself in the stickiest situations—with any stud whose path he crosses! His adventures with "The Demon of Death" promise another carnal carnival.

The Adventures of Miles Diamond $4.95/118-7

"The Case of the Missing Twin" promises to be a most rewarding case, packed as it is with randy studs. Miles sets about uncovering all as he tracks down the elusive and delectable Daniel Travis....

KELVIN BELIELE

If the Shoe Fits $4.95/223-X

An essential and winning volume of tales exploring a world where randy boys can't help but do what comes naturally—as often as possible! Sweaty male bodies grapple in pleasure, proving the old adage: if the shoe fits, one might as well slip right in....

VICTOR TERRY

WHiPs $4.95/254-X

Connoisseurs of gay writing have known Victor Terry's work for some time. Cruising for a hot man? You'd better be, because one way or another, these WHiPs—officers of the Wyoming Highway Patrol—are gonna pull you over for a little impromptu interrogation....

MAX EXANDER

Deeds of the Night: Tales of Eros and Passion $5.95/348-1

MAXimum porn! Exander's a writer who's seen it all—and is more than happy to describe every inch of it in pulsating detail. From the man behind *Mansex* and *Leathersex*—two whirlwind tours of the hypermasculine libido—comes another unrestrained volume of sweat-soaked fantasies.

ORDERING IS EASY!

MC/VISA orders can be placed by calling our toll-free number

PHONE 800 375-2356/FAX 212 986-7355

or mail the coupon below to:

MASQUERADE BOOKS
DEPT. X74A, 801 SECOND AVENUE, NY, NY 10017

BUY ANY FOUR BOOKS AND CHOOSE ONE ADDITIONAL BOOK, OF EQUAL OR LESSER VALUE, AS YOUR FREE GIFT.

QTY.	TITLE	NO.	PRICE
			FREE
			FREE

X74A

SUBTOTAL

POSTAGE and HANDLING

We Never Sell, Give or Trade Any Customer's Name.

TOTAL

In the U.S., please add $1.50 for the first book and 75¢ for each additional book; in Canada, add $2.00 for the first book and $1.25 for each additional book. Foreign countries: add $4.00 for the first book and $2.00 for each additional book. No C.O.D. orders. Please make all checks payable to Masquerade Books. Payable in U.S. currency only. New York state residents add 8¼% sales tax. Please allow 4-6 weeks delivery.

NAME

ADDRESS

CITY_____ STATE_____ ZIP_____

TEL (   )

PAYMENT: ☐ CHECK   ☐ MONEY ORDER   ☐ VISA   ☐ MC

CARD NO._____ EXP. DATE_____